# MÉRIDA

JOSÉ Mª ÁLVAREZ MARTÍNEZ
JOSÉ LUIS DE LA BARRERA ANTÓN
AGUSTÍN VELÁZQUEZ JIMÉNEZ

**EVEREST**

**Photographs:** Manuel de la Barrera Ocaña

**Design and Layout:** Gerardo Rodera

**Translated by:** EURO:TEXT

**Cover Design:** Alfredo Anievas

THIRD EDITION
© José Mª Álvarez Martínez
   José Luis de la Barrera Antón
   Agustín Velázquez Jiménez
   EDITORIAL EVEREST, S.A.
Carretera León-La Coruña, km 5 - LEÓN
ISBN-Number: 84-241-3806-6
Legal deposit: LE. 14-2000
Printed in Spain

EDITORIAL EVERGRÁFICAS, S.L.
Carretera León-La Coruña, km 5
LEON (Spain)

# MÉRIDA

## HISTORICAL INTRODUCTION

The oldest remains that have been found in Mérida and its surrounding area date back to the Lower Palaeolithic. However, all evidence would seem to indicate that there was no true occupation of this territory until the late Neolithic. Indeed it is to this period of time, around 3000-2000 B.C., that the remains of a small settlement discovered in the present-day *Avenida de Juan Carlos I* are to be attributed. The said remains were almost completely destroyed by a Roman necropolis that was erected on the same site nearly three thousand years later.

Excavations have been carried out at a number of settlements dating from this period situated in the environs of Mérida, bringing to light the important status achieved by the area at the very end of the Neolithic and in the Chalcolithic or Copper Age. Examples of such settlements are *Cueva de La Charneca, Araya* and *La Palacina.*

The most outstanding prehistoric monument, however, is the *Dolmen de Lácara,* a magnificent megalithic sepulchre which has been declared a National Monument and is located amidst the typical meadowland scenery of Extremadura. It constitutes a characteristic type of dolmen, featuring as it does a large chamber and a long corridor divided into sections, the entire construction having been covered in its day by an enormous artificial mound of stones and earth that in former times would have been clearly visible.

We also have knowledge of widely scattered remains belonging to the Bronze and Stone Ages, some of which were found in Mérida itself, others having been discovered at sites in the surrounding area. Worthy of mention here are a number of culturally very significant objects, such as the golden earrings and anklets that go to make up the so-called "Treasure of Mérida" that is kept at the British Museum in London and which is to be dated as belonging to the Late Bronze Age. Likewise housed in the British Museum is a curious little bronze figure which, representing a Phoenician-style warrior, dates back to around the 7th century B.C., in other words, to the time when the cultural influence of the Greeks and the Phoenicians was felt all over the southern part of the Iberian peninsula.

Of somewhat later origin (6th-5th centuries B.C.) is another most peculiar item, namely the so-called *"carrito de Mérida"* or little chariot of Mérida, kept at the Museum of Saint Germain-en-Laye in Paris. Clearly votive in nature, this is yet another indication of the impact of Mediterranean and oriental influences on this area. Other finds that have been made would seem to point in the same direction, including as they do *kernos* and Iberian votive offerings. However, there is no evidence to urrefutably confirm the existence in Mérida of a Pre-Roman settlement or fortification. In times prior to the foundation of the Roman town, the territory in which Mérida is situated today constituted a border zone or a point of contact between the Vettones and the Turdetani, although the area was also prone to invasion by the war-hungry Lusitanian peoples. The native population of Roman Mérida was therefore surely composed of groups of Turdetani, Vettones and Lusitanians.

To quote Dion Cassius (155-235 A.D.) from his *Historia Romana* (53,25,2), "Once the war was over (that fought by Rome against the Cantabri and the Astures), Augustus discharged the most veteran of his soldiers and granted them permission to found a city called Emerita Augusta in the province of Lusitania".

Similar words were to be employed centuries later in turn by Saint Isidore of Seville in his work entitled *Etymologiae* (15,1,69).

These two texts constitute the principal documentary sources that enlighten us as to the foundation of the colony called Emerita Augusta. In

3

**1.** *Pebble tool.*

part of the peninsula with a series of *praesidia* or fortified towns such as those at *Metellium* (Medellín), *Norba* (Cáceres), *Scallabis* (Santarem), *Pax Iulia* (Beja), to name but a few. It is indeed to be considered very surprising that no notice was taken of the location constituting the subject of this book and that this territory, from which control could be exercised over all the existing trade routes, should have been ignored, above all by Caesar, who himself was such a great strategist and topographer.

According to information to be gleaned from the coins issued by the mint at Emerita Augusta, the veteran soldiers that came to settle here were those released from the V Legion *Alaudae* and X Legion *Gemina,* although it is also highly probable that some of them had also served in the XX Legion *Victoria Victrix.*

Publio Carisio, a general who had taken part in the wars against the Astures, was designated legate and maximum authority of the new settlement. However, a number of archaeological finds have enlightened us as to the fact that the *factotum,* the true master of the colony, was to be no other than Marco Vipsanio Agrippa.

The idea that lay behind the foundation of Emerita Augusta was that of constructing a fortified town and at the same time offering tangible proof of the advantages of Romanization *(speculum ac propugnaculum imperii romani).*

Thus the fledgling colony was to become a strategic enclave amidst lands that had not been fully subdued and which were in principle somewhat opposed to the idea of Romanization. Its strategic value was determined by the fact that this was the point at which the course of the River Guadiana entered a favourable tract of land, over which a bridge was projected to bring the lands of Baetica into contact with the very troublesome northern and north-western areas of the peninsula that were of such great importance to the Roman public treasury.

Having inherited the rôle that at the outset had been played by Medellín, the new colony was to become, in the light of the new conquests, the epicentre of Roman policy in the Iberian peninsula. The fact was that Emerita, together with its extensive surrounding territory, was in direct contact with the other provinces, Tarraconensis and Baetica, and as a result soon constituted an important focal point of the communications network, as it were at the crossroads of the western peninsula.

In all likelihood the veterans were joined in their mission by the indigenous people, who, according to Estrabón, to a certain extent became involved in the

addition, the efforts of archaeologists have provided us with further evidence that throws light on certain aspects of those early days of the town´s history, such as the identity of its settlers, the authorities that were delegated at its foundation, the structure of the town and the nature of its first monuments.

In the light of the above sources, it is generally agreed that the foundation of Emerita Augusta must have taken place in the year 25 B.C., subsequent to the conclusion of one of the episodes in the wars waged by Rome against the indomitable Cantabri and Astures, an episode that was marked by the capture of Lancia. Nevertheless, some authors prefer the later date of 19 B.C., the point in time when the Cantabrian wars finally came to an end.

In spite of all this, and even if we are to accept the year 25 B.C. as that which saw the creation of the colony of Emerita Augusta, the truth still remains that the strategic position *par excellence* that we have already referred to with regard to this site was totally overlooked by the "Roman eye" that had strewn this new situation, thus giving rise to a sector of the population which can be described as being semi-military in nature.

At a later date, once the town itself had been consolidated, Emerita would be designated the capital of the newly-formed province of Lusitania.

Whilst the political, military, social and administrative motives underlying the colony´s foundation were plain for all to see, no less obvious were the reasons of a topographical nature. The topography of the Mérida area has two main features, namely the River Guadiana and the gently rising hills on which the town was established.

As was the case with so many of the towns of antiquity, *Emerita Augusta* owed its birth to the existence of a river. The Mérida area was quite simply the only place for miles around at which the Anas (as the Guadiana was known in Roman times) could be crossed on foot with relative ease. If to this we add the fact that there was an island in the middle of the channel, it is easy to comprehend the great strategic value of the town.

The importance of the trade routes was also a vital factor and the need to control the roads determined the choice of the site on which a new town should be constructed. The great significance of the Roman roads is to be seen in the fact that the main streets of any town were formed by these thoroughfares themselves or were continuations of the same. This was the case in *Emerita,* where the *decumanus maximus* was in fact the road which, originating in the south of the peninsula, headed for the high plateau or meseta, and the *kardo maximus* was to a large extent none other than the north-western road.

When the location of Emerita was to be decided, the Guadiana island, together with the shallow waters that made it possible to cross the river at this point, was seen to outweigh all other possibilities. A long bridge was built spanning the whole width of the channel, thus allowing for a free passage of the river.

The exact site chosen for the emplacement of the town was the right bank of the river, which, in spite of the fact that it entailed a few difficulties, appeared to be the best suited. The major problem was presented by the enormous swellings of the river flow that were witnessed in ancient times, a fact reflected by the restoration of the bridge in the Visigothic era. In order to avoid such potential devastation and to reinforce the very slight protection offered by the elevation the river terrace, the Roman colonists constructed a strong rubblework dyke with ashlar buttresses right along the riverbank. Such a defence provided the inhabitants of Emerita with protection from the floods which,

according to ancient sources, wrought havoc in Rome itself and many other cities of the Empire.

The dyke itself is a prodigious construction praised highly by Moreno de Vargas, who in his well-known work recounts the astonishment of Philip II and his architect Juan de Herrera on beholding it during their stay in Mérida.

Whereas the difficulties and disadvantages involved in establishing the town on the right bank of the river Guadiana were minimal and were easily overcome, the advantages that such an emplacement entailed were enormous.

On the one hand, this particular area - in contrast to the opposite bank - had an abundant supply of water. A large number of springs have been discovered within the perimeters of what was the Roman colony and today it is still possible to see some of the reservoirs that were built in order to exploit this natural resource. Moreover, appropriate geological explorations of this land have confirmed the fact that a series of depressions once existed alongside several streams and other water channels. It was in this way

**2.** *Schematic cave-painting at La Calderita.*

**3.** *An as featuring a yoke of oxen and a priest plotting out the original site of the town´s foundation.*

that, on exploiting the available natural resources, the Romans were able to set up the three water-carrying conduits of Emerita Augusta, namely the "Cornalvo" *(Aqua Augusta),* "Rabo de Buey-San Lázaro" and "Proserpina" aqueducts.

Furthermore, the topographical situation of this area afforded the town a number of well-aired hills that provided the perfect site for the construction of important edifices. Thus, on the high ground surrounding the San Albín Hill it was possible to erect, in a "Greek style" and with all the inherent advantages, the rising tiers of seats belonging to the theatre and part of those of the neighbouring amphitheatre.

Last but not least, the site chosen for the colony was one well-suited to defence, a fact which enabled the town walls, which were laid out following the rolling contours of the hills, to be solidly built.

Furthermore, agriculturally speaking the Mérida plains were then and still are today a high quality area, featuring as they do land suitable for farming, pastures for the grazing of livestock, not to mention an abundance of game.

The extensive mineral resources of the area have also become a matter of common knowledge, thanks to the magnificent study carried out by that most distinguished figure in Mérida, Vicente Sos Baynat.

Indeed it can be said that here the Romans had at their disposal all the materials that were necessary for the construction of the new town, namely marbles, granites, diorites, sands, gravels, etc.

The new colony was bestowed with extensive lands which, if we were to use a modern-day term somewhat lacking in precision, we could call its "municipal district". The liberal fashion in which the said lands were shared out was certainly out of keeping with the common practice of those times.

However, in spite of the valuable but rather incomplete information provided by surveyors, we still have a long way to go before we can ascertain the ultimate shape this colony was to take. Whilst it is true that the boundaries marking the limits of the area pertaining to Emerita Augusta can be defined fairly convincingly, one has to admit that very little is known with regard to the exact structure of this colonial territory or *ager,* the way in which Roman centuries were deployed here, its viability or its demographic distribution.

We can also confirm that the said territory, measuring as it did almost 20,000 square kilometres, was divided into three prefectures or administrative areas. Its borders reached as far as the Norba territory in the north, the *conventus hispalensis y cordubensis* in the south, Valdecaballeros in the east and the marble quarries of the Borba and Estremoz area in the west.

This territory, that boasted excellent farming and pasture land, an abundance of mining and quarry deposits and whose viability was determined by a road network uniting its various settlements, was to witness a flourishing of economic activity throughout the Roman era, an activity which in turn marked the development of the colony of Emerita Augusta.

Although we are in possession of a relatively large amount of information as regards the determining factors that influenced the foundation of the colony, our knowledge of the historical evolution of the latter is practically non-existent.

We can only imagine that, as was the case with the whole of Hispania, the advent of the Flavian dynasty was to entail a great impulse for the construction of monumental architecture in Emerita Augusta, an impulse which doubtless had some connection with the previous arrival, under the rule of Emperor Otho, of a new influx of population. The new citizens, who on this occasion originated entirely from Italica, were to inject new lifeblood into Emerita, a town which at that time was perhaps only partially occupied but whose population would soon reach the considerable figure of 25,000 inhabitants.

In its rôle as a prime centre of communications (a total of nine main roads were to lead off from Emerita, uniting the latter with the most important cities of the Empire), Emerita Augusta was an important stage on what was subsequently to become known as the "Silver Route" (iter ab Emerita Asturicam) which connected Seville and the Atlantic coast with the semi-Romanized lands of the north of the peninsula. Furthermore, the town was to undergo such economic, commercial and industrial development which meant that, apart from being the administrative capital of the extensive province of Lusitania, it became one of the highest-ranking centres of political activity. Under the aid and protection of the provincial governor, supported as he was by an immense bureaucratic apparatus, cultural life flourished and a demand arose for the provision of basic necessities. Consequently, Emerita attracted the major artists and craftsmen of the Empire who were to fashion their best creations here, some of which are on display at the Museum of Mérida.

No record is held regarding the impact on Emerita of the often referred to "crisis" of the 3rd century, neither is there any archaeological evidence that bears witness to such an event. On the contrary, we have sufficient proof that right from the early years of the 4th century, coinciding with the advent of the dynasty

**4.** *Mérida pitcher.*

of Constantine, the town experienced another period of revival. A pair of epigraphic monuments dating from this time inform us as to the reconstruction of the two most significant buildings dedicated to public entertainment, namely the theatre and the circus. These constructions had fallen into decay with the passing of time *(vetustate conlapsum),* and were recovered for their original purpose thanks to the generosity of Constantine and his sons. The administration of the Emperor´s donations for the reconstruction process was supervised by the governor of the entire *dioccsis Hispaniarum* who, as a result of the latest administrative reform, had set up residence in Mérida.

A few years earlier, Emerita had held the dubious distinction of being mentioned in the chronicles on account of the martyrdom of St Eulalie (303), an active member of the town´s doubtless extremely numerous and problematic Christian community. The hierarchical organization of the latter goes back at least as far as the time of the persecution of Christians under

**5.** *San Lázaro Aqueduct from an engraving by Laborde.*

Decius (3rd century), in the course of which the town is reported to have rejected its bishop, Marcial, whom it accused of avoiding persecution by renouncing his faith and thus obtaining a certificate of apostasy.

Subsequent to the Milan Edict of Toleration that granted freedom of worship (313), Mérida was to become one of the three Spanish cities, along with Seville and Tarragona, that were conferred the status of archdiocese. In fact the jurisdiction of the archbishop of Mérida encompassed a total of 12 episcopal sees and the resulting power wielded by the archbishopric, which was not exclusively of a spiritual nature, was to prove to be an important catalyst for the urban development of the town, which was soon to rank high on the list of the major cities of the Roman world. This achievement was acclaimed by the poet Marco Ausonio (second half of the 4th century) in his *ordo nobilium urbium,* according to which Emerita was assigned ninth place amongst the seventeen most important cities of the Empire.

Once the first wave of invasions of Empire territory had been undertaken by the peoples from the north of the peninsula, Mérida –and Lusitania as a whole– became the scene for conflicts between the Suevi, the Alans and the Vandals, all of whom were willing to fight in order to take control of the void that was left by the disappearance of imperial authority.

We learn from the traditional sources that in around 409 the Alans occupied Lusitania and shortly afterwards mingled with the Vandals who had settled in Baetica. These two peoples joined forces and, in a battle that took place near Mérida, clashed with the

Suevi, who were completely vanquished and lost their king, the latter having drowned in the River Guadiana. Not long afterwards, in 442, once the Vandals had crossed into Africa, the Sueve Rechila occupied Mérida after having defeated the imperial army. Rechila was to establish the capital of his kingdom here and in 457 further secured his dominion on defeating the Visigoths, who in vain tried to recover the town on behalf of the Romans.

Once the imperial authority had completely disappeared, the Visigoths seized control of the town in 469. Mérida thus became the capital of one of the six constituent provinces of Hispania and provided the residence for the *dux* who governed the land. During the reign of Agila, Mérida was to attain the status of capital of the Visigothic kingdom, a privilege that owing to political interests was later to be transferred to Toledo.

*Emeritensium* and attributed to Paul the Deacon, we have come to know of the flourishing economic and commercial activity that prevailed in Mérida at that time. Such enterprise was promoted to a large extent by the efforts of the town´s archbishops, who effectively came to take over the function of the civil authority. Moreover it was with the same enthusiasm that they set about the construction of monasteries and basilicas, the building of schools and hospitals, and the provision of funds for the establishment of credit institutions to lend money at low interest to the most needy sections of the population. The architectural remains belonging to this period that have been found up to date, providing as they do such a vividly expressive testimony to the flourishing of the arts and culture, have led more than one scholar to conclude –perhaps rather exaggeratedly– that Mérida was the birthplace of Visigothic art.

**6.** *Inscription which, dating from the rule of Constantine, alludes to the reconstruction of the circus.*

At the time when Hermengild rose up in rebellion against his father, the feelings of the Hispano-Roman substratum of the population and the opinion held by the bishops of Mérida, the latter being true bastions of orthodoxy, were to exert a great influence on the decision of the orthodox forces to openly support the rebellious son in his cause. Consequently, the town was to feel in its very own flesh the effects of the violent battles fought against the Arian Royal Army and the reprisals taken by the civil authority against the head of the local Catholic clergy, Masona, a figure who was later to be fully recognized, once the ruler Reccared had undergone conversion to the faith.

By virtue of an opuscule dating from the 7th century entitled *De vita et miraculis Patrum*

As legend will have it, after their defeat at the hands of the Moslem forces at Guadalete (711), the remainder of the vanquished Visigothic army took refuge in Mérida, where under the leadership of Rodrigo they held out for over a year under siege from the Moors. Once the siege was over, a pact was agreed with the victorious Moslem leader Muza, according to which the latter proceeded to occupy the town in a peaceful manner and the inhabitants were allowed to both maintain their prevailing civil organization and to continue enjoying their traditional rights.

Although at first the Moslem conquest was accepted not overreluctantly by the inhabitants of Mérida, tired as they were of the internal conflicts of the Gothic nobles, it was not to be long before the

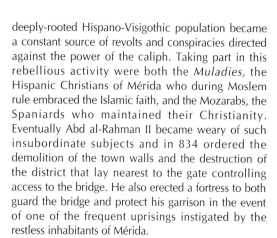

7. *A dupondius minted in Mérida and featuring the town gate.*

8. *Visigothic coin struck in Mérida.*

deeply-rooted Hispano-Visigothic population became a constant source of revolts and conspiracies directed against the power of the caliph. Taking part in this rebellious activity were both the *Muladies,* the Hispanic Christians of Mérida who during Moslem rule embraced the Islamic faith, and the Mozarabs, the Spaniards who maintained their Christianity. Eventually Abd al-Rahman II became weary of such insubordinate subjects and in 834 ordered the demolition of the town walls and the destruction of the district that lay nearest to the gate controlling access to the bridge. He also erected a fortress to both guard the bridge and protect his garrison in the event of one of the frequent uprisings instigated by the restless inhabitants of Mérida.

Such instability doubtless led to a mass exodus of the population and a dramatic decline in the town's overall importance, so much so that on the eclipse of the Umayyad caliphate, the *"taifa"* kingdom that replaced it was to set up its capital in neighbouring Badajoz. However, the many years of skirmishes, sackings and despoliation did not suffice to conceal Mérida's magnificent past, and before the end of the 9th century the Moor Rasis was prompted to write: "...And I tell you that there is no man in the whole world whose words could do full justice to the marvels of Mérida".

Whilst the period of Arab domination had had a detrimental effect on Mérida –a fact confirmed by local historians– it is no less true that the Christian *reconquista* simply could not have had a worse beginning for the former provincial capital. Indeed, this was the first historical opportunity for Mérida to recuperate its past glory, an opportunity that was to vanish when, after the town had been conquered by the Christian forces under Alfonso IX of León on 10th January 1230, Mérida was subjected to the authority of the archbishop of Santiago de Compostela. Previously, by means of a papal bull issued by Callistus II on 26th February 1120 and in accordance with the wishes of Alfonso VII, the town of Santiago had obtained for itself the transfer of the archbishopric that had belonged to Mérida. To further complicate matters, a few years later Diego Gelmírez, the archbishop of Santiago, fearing a future resurgence of Mérida and the latter's claim for the return of its former ecclesiastical status, had conferred the dominion of Mérida to the Order of St James, whilst himself maintaining religious jurisdiction over the town, in exchange for some of the possessions held by the Order in Galicia. Consequently, Mérida was to remain under the command of the Order of St James until the time when the lands of such military orders were brought under the control of the Crown.

After having attempted in vain on several occasions to regain its archiepiscopal see, for a long time Mérida was a town of no great significance, playing no part in the shaping of history. Nevertheless, it was strategically situated at the crossroads of all the main trade routes of the Crown and bore silent witness to the comings and goings of the many travellers that passed the town, both from north to south and from east to west. Such was the state of affairs until the advent of the Catholic Kings, when the first signs of Mérida´s economic recovery were to be seen, a situation eloquently reflected by the buildings, both of a civil and a religious nature, that came to adorn the town, and amongst which we can cite the *Sala del Concejo* or Council Hall, the Palace of Los Corbos, that of La Roca and the Santa Eulalia and Santa María parish churches.

As had previously been the case on occasion of the wars waged against Portugal in 1382 and 1430 by John I and John II of Castile respectively, the Mérida area was later once again to reluctantly become, due to its strategic position, the scene of bloody skirmishes, this time between the supporters of Isabella and those loyal to Juana *la Beltraneja,* in the dispute over which of the two princesses should succeed to the throne of Castile. In fact it was in the vicinity of Mérida, to be precise in La Albuera, that a decisive battle would take place, one that was to virtually tip the scales of the struggle in favour of Isabella and Ferdinand, and in the course of which the master of Santiago Alonso de Cárdenas was to distinguish himself as a result of his valour. This outcome, however, did not prevent the town from remaining for some time in the hands of the war-hungry Doña Beatriz Pacheco, the Countess of Medellín. Once peace was finally brought to the region, a comprehensive programme of reconstruction and embellishment was undertaken in Mérida which encompassed not only the palaces and churches, but also the Roman bridge, which owing to its strategic position had constituted the target for attacks perpetrated by both sides involved in the dispute.

It is to be assumed that, during the reign of the first Habsburg monarchs of Spain, Mérida continued its slow, unremarkable process of recovery, although the records we possess on this period are few and far between, mostly lack any form of historical interest and are merely of anecdotal value. There is no extant document that either proves or disproves the participation of the Council of Mérida in the War of the *Comunidades,* and there is but one record of the fleeting visit in 1526 of King Charles I, who was on his way to Seville, where he would marry Isabella of Portugal.

In 1557, Mérida made preparations –in the utmost solemnity– to receive the mortal remains of the emperor´s sister, Eleanor of Austria, queen of Portugal and France. Eleanor had died in Talavera and was buried in Mérida at the Church of Santa María.

**9.** *Painting inside a Roman columbarium, or recess for cinerary urns.*

Subsequently, in 1574, her remains were transferred to El Escorial. Years later, in 1580, it was the turn of Philip II to stay awhile in Mérida whilst he planned the annexation of Portugal. In 1619, the chronicles of Mérida reported, in a joyous tone, both the visit paid on 4th May by King Philip III en route to Portugal, and the festivities held in honour of such an illustrious guest.

Whilst on the one hand we may indeed uphold the view purported by the local scholar Vicente Navarro Castillo that the reign of the first Spanish-

**10.** *Aerial view of Mérida.* ▶
*(Photograph: Jesús Rueda).*

Habsburg monarchs brought about an era of great social and economic development in Mérida, on the other hand we must not overlook the fact that the policies of Philip IV served only to inspire despair and were to entail catastrophic consequences for the town. During his reign, the popular uprisings in Catalonia and Portugal were indeed to have serious repercussions on the entire Mérida area. Above all the proximity of Portugal meant that this area was called upon, over a period of twenty long years, to act as an inexhaustible source of men, provisions and money to fuel the king's attempt to suppress the revolt. The ultimate outcome for Mérida was the exodus of its inhabitants, many of whom fled the town for fear of conscription, compulsory billeting and the confiscation of their possessions. It should come as no surprise, therefore, that upon the conclusion of hostilities in 1668 those contemporary travellers who had cause to pass through Mérida could find no other words to describe the town than those of "ruined", "poor" and "abandoned".

Not even the advent of the Bourbon dynasty would lead to an improvement in the living conditions of the people of Mérida. No sooner had Philip V been proclaimed king in 1700 than the War of the Spanish Succession broke out. Mérida itself was to remain fairly removed from the conflict until 1704, when an Anglo-Dutch army landed in Portugal and attempted to invade Spain via the Extremadura frontier. From this point in time on, in a process that lasted up until 1709, Mérida was to witness the repetition of the calamitous events of the 17th century, its surrounding area being ravaged and plundered as a result of the battles and skirmishes fought by the warring forces. Further havoc was thus wrought in the depleted local economy, an economy that was still recovering from the disasters that had struck in the previous century.

With reference to the reigns of Charles III and Charles IV, the town chronicles inform us of the visit paid to Mérida by the queen of Portugal, on her way to Madrid to have talks with King Charles III, and that of Charles IV and his wife, who stopped here en route to Badajoz, where they were to spend a few days in the company of the royal favourite, Manuel Godoy, in 1796. Meanwhile, the philosophical movement prevailing at this time was the Enlightenment, which, personified in the figure of the Count of Campomanes, was to entail a resurgence of the agricultural and industrial activity of the town. This revival was part of a trend that had swept right across Spain, but a few years later it was to be abruptly brought to an end by the War of Independence.

The truth is that Mérida, as was the case with practically all Spanish towns, was not to be spared from the ravages of this war. As early as 31st March 1809, French troops under the command of Marshall Victor entered the town, meeting no resistance on their way. They proceeded to plunder both the local wheat granary and the Church of *Santa Eulalia* and departed shortly afterwards, not to return until 1810. However, it was in 1811 that from artillery posts lying within Mérida itself the Spanish forces engaged in a fierce battle against the invading troops who had taken up their positions on the outskirts of the town. In the aftermath of the battle more than twenty five percent of the urban fabric of Mérida lay in ruins and large sections of the population had abandoned the town for the country. In 1812, Mérida, or what was left of it, silently looked on as the French troops beat their retreat, not however before they had pillaged sites of archaeological importance, as we are reminded by the chronicles of the day.

During the reign of Ferdinand VII, the year 1823 saw the arrival in Mérida of yet another contingent of French troops, which on this occasion had been sent by the king himself and were on the march to Seville in order to impose the absolute power of the sovereign.

Once this age of uncertainty and surprise had drawn to a close, and since Mérida was not to be involved in the subsequent outbursts of civil unrest, the town entered a stage of its history characterized by slow but steady economic growth. The decisive impulse for this development was provided by the inclusion of Mérida in the Spanish railway network in 1862, an event which would simultaneously lead to an increase in the town's population and the resulting extension of the urban centre right through the first third of the 19th century. This slow but continuous process of revival undergone by Mérida, the momentum of which would only be checked by the most recent of Spanish civil wars and the consequent post-war penury, was to be intensified by the rapid development that took place in the 1950s and which saw Mérida slowly transform into an industry and service-oriented town, thus adding to its traditional rôle as a focal point in the peninsula's communications network. Amongst the noteworthy features of Mérida's recent history, we should perhaps highlight the following: the initiation, in the second decade of the present century, of a series of systematic excavation campaigns at Mérida's ensemble of ancient monuments which has continued almost uninterruptedly right up to the present day; the restoration of the monuments themselves and the

**11.** *A view of Mérida taken from an engraving by De Laborde.*

promotion of the town's archaeological heritage, which today comes under the protection of the *Junta* or Regional Government of Extremadura; the proclamation of Mérida as an Historical-Archaeological Ensemble by virtue of a Royal Decree issued on 8th February 1973; and finally the creation of the New National Museum of Roman Art, opened by their Highnesses the King and Queen of Spain on 19th September 1986. As a result of the above-mentioned efforts, Mérida has evolved into one of the primary tourist centres of Spain, a fact confirmed by the several hundreds of thousands of visitors that come to the town in the course of a year.

Lastly, having been designated capital of the Autonomous Community of Extremadura and seat of both the Autonomous Government and the Regional Parliament, Mérida has become a centre of administration and services, and has thus at last regained the rôle it had been deprived of for one and a half millennia. Present-day Mérida, totalling around 60,000 inhabitants and boasting first-class tourist and hotel amenities together with a wide spectrum of services, has managed to harmoniously combine the past and the present and looks to the future with great hope and optimism, conscious of its past glory and aware of the brilliant future that lies ahead.

# PRE-ROMAN MÉRIDA

Taking into account the sheer extent of the urban development carried out by the Romans in Mérida, it should come as no surprise that in order to come across the most significant evidence bearing witness to the activity of Pre-Roman peoples in the Mérida area, we have to venture outside the town limits. Consequently, we would suggest that the visitor undertake a visit to the *Dolmen de Lácara* and the prehistoric paintings to be seen both at La Calderita and in the mountains at Arroyo de San Serván.

15

**12.** *Dolmen de Lácara.*

### THE MEGALITHIC TOMB AT LÁCARA

The megalithic sepulchre at Lácara, which was declared a National Monument in 1931, ranks as one of the most spectacular sights to be seen in the whole of Extremadura and constitutes an excellent example of megalithic architecture in the west of the Iberian peninsula. This particular dolmen is to be classified amongst those featuring a long corridor and a circular chamber. In its structure one can clearly appreciate the three elements so characteristic of such burial monuments, namely its circular chamber measuring 5.1 metres in diameter, its corridor, which, having a length of 20 metres, is divided into three sections, and finally the mound of earth and stones that had once covered the whole construction. The dolmen stands 3.5 metres tall and takes the shape of an ellipse whose longest axis measures 35 metres.

The monument was constructed by sinking large blocks of stone into the earth. Tall stones were reserved for the chamber, whilst smaller ones were used to build the corridor, covered as they were by massive, relatively even slabs that provided an irregular flat roof. Having been erected for funerary purposes, the dolmen was to house collective burials, bodies being interred along with certain simple personal belongings, such as pottery, stone tools, ornaments and metal objects. In fact it is these very objects, unearthed in the course of the excavations led by Almagro Basch and now on display at the Museum of Badajoz, that have come to show us that the tomb was re-used in the Bronze Age for exactly the same purpose.

*Dolmen de Lácara* is to be reached by following the N 630 road out of Mérida and, on passing the village of Aljucén, taking the local road leading to La Nava de Santiago. You will see signs for the monument a few kilometres after the turning.

### CAVE PAINTINGS AT LA CALDERITA

The essential features of the schematic rock painting typical of the southern Iberian peninsula are to be observed at the cave locally referred to as *El abrigo de la Calderita*. Here we find a variety of figures, whose forms are indeed highly schematic and which have each been created using a single hue of red. Particularly noteworthy are the representations of idols and anthropomorphic beings that feature insinuations of eyes, arms and suns, and which do not appear to constitute any kind of scene, but rather portray graphic stereotypes whose meaning is unknown but whose symbology is comparable to that of the idols and ceramic ornaments of the Chalcolithic period. As is the case with almost all such sites of cave art, La Calderita looks out over an expanse of mountains sweeping down to the peneplain below.

The cave is to be found in the *Peñas Blancas* mountain range, lying between the villages of Alange and Zarza de Alange. It is easily reached by means of the local road that leads from Mérida to the said villages.

## THE SAN SERVÁN ENSEMBLE OF CAVE ART

The San Serván ensemble of cave art encompasses over thirty sites of rock paintings situated all over the mountain range. They display a great variety of motifs, amongst which the most frequent are those of anthropomorphic beings, idols, quadrupeds, suns, and bars. There is even what could possibly be a cart, a highly interesting motif since it indicates the late date at which it was painted and lends support to the theory that this particular art form perdured over an extensive period of time spanning the Chalcolithic, the Bronze Age and the beginnings of the Iron Age.

Amongst the anthropomorphic figures to be seen, the most striking are those portrayed with their hands on their hips, along with other figures called "swallows" due to the fact that their outlines are very reminiscent of these birds, and the so-called bi-triangular forms. The most remarkable idols are those featuring pronounced eyes, whilst the quadrupeds are normally depicted in the form of canids, sheep and goats and on occasions deer, the latter being recognizable due to the insinuation of the animals´ horns.

These paintings are scattered all over the San Serván mountain range, which itself is to be reached by following the N-V road and turning off along the local road leading to the village of Arroyo de San Serván.

# ROMAN MÉRIDA

## TOPOGRAPHY AND URBAN DEVELOPMENT OF ROMAN MÉRIDA

The foundation of the Roman colony *Emerita Augusta,* an event which in all probability took place in the year 25 B.C., was carried out *ex novo,* that is to say, on a site that up to then had not been occupied by a settlement of any significance. It is quite feasible, however, that the hill referred to as "El Calvario", commanding as it does a particularly strategic position, bound on either side by the rivers Guadiana and Albarregas, could have been previously graced by a small *castellum* or castle, the purpose of which would have been to observe and control any crossings of the river at a point where the latter was easily forded.

Subsequently, during the period of the town´s foundation, this shallow section of the river facilitated the construction of the supports of a long bridge that was to both determine the exact location of the town and define the urban layout of the latter, since one of the major arteries of the new settlement, the *decumanus maximus,* was in fact a prolongation of the road that led across the bridge.

In spite of the obvious difficulties that arise in any study of the topography and urban development of *Emerita,* due to the fact that the ancient town has effectively been overlaid by the modern one, recent research has made it possible to draw up an approximate outline of the urban fabric of the colony.

Two basic theories have been put forward with regard to the urban aspect of the Roman town. The first of these theories, upheld by the researchers Schulten, Mélida, Gil Farrés, García y Bellido and others, postulates that on its foundation Emerita must have formed what can be termed an initial nucleus, the limits of which were marked by the *Puerta del Puente,* or bridge gate, and the *Puerta de la Villa,* or town gate, situated on the *decumanus maximus* and the Trajan and Cimbron arches at either end of the *kardo maximus.*

Thus, if we are to go by these hypothetical boundaries derived basically from the plan of the drains serving the road network, it would seem that in its earliest form Mérida covered an area of 350 square metres and would subsequently double in size to measure the equivalent of 49 hectares.

**13.** *Group of Roman columbaria.*

On undertaking an in-depth study of this theory –a theory which was elaborated at a time when the "square town" concept dominated all study of ancient urban development– we are forced to reject it for a number of reasons.

Even though the limits set out for the *decumanus maximus* may well be accurate, the same cannot be maintained of those of the *kardo maximus,* since the so-called *Arco de Trajano* (Trajan´s Arch) was not one of the town´s gates, but rather an arch forming the entrance to a sacred area, and there is no proof of the existence of the *Arco del Cimbrón.* Moreover, if this theory were true, Mérida´s public place, or forum, in which the ruins of the Temple of Diana are to be found, would have been situated not at the heart of the sacred area but rather on the periphery of the latter, partly projecting beyond the same.

Today the most generally favoured of the two theories is the second one, according to which *Emerita* was a town of large proportions encircled right from the very beginning by a wall, and, just as is the case with modern-day housing estates, it included a series of "open spaces" which in time would gradually be occupied at a rate proportionate to the need for expansion resulting from the town´s growth.

This theory was drawn up by the English researcher Richmond, who amongst other important factors noticed that the fabric of the Amphitheatre –dating from 8 A.D.– actually rested on the walled enclosure, as a result of which he deemed the latter to logically have existed prior to the construction of the former. He also pointed out that the "Cornalvo"

aqueduct, whose construction is likewise to be assigned to the early days of the town´s history, had been erected along the top of the town wall itself.

Emerita Augusta, therefore, is to be seen as yet another example of the way in which towns were conceived during the reign of emperor Augustus, towns that were planned with a view to the future and which right from the outset were designed on a large scale.

Highly evocative remains of the town wall are to be found in several parts of Mérida. A series of excavations undertaken at the wall´s foundations have confirmed that it was built in the early years of the colony´s existence. Thanks to the evidence gathered by the local historian Moreno de Vargas, it is possible to retrace the course taken by the wall around the town. The perimeter of the wall, whose layout is seen to have been totally conditioned by topographical factors, is trapezoidal in shape. We have perfect knowledge with regard to one of the town gates that were situated at either end of the main thoroughfares,

**14.** *Painting inside a Roman columbarium, or recess for cinerary urns.*

**15.** *Roman road.*

namely the *Puerta del Puente* or Bridge Gate, which the visitor to Mérida can admire within the grounds of the *Alcazaba* or Citadel. The structure of this gate matches that which is portrayed on the coins issued by the Mérida mint, and features a double opening set between two rounded towers. It is clear that a series of minor gates, or *portillos,* also existed in the wall, above all on the riverside façade of the latter. Every so often the fabric of the wall would be divided into sections by round-shaped towers.

In time the extension of Mérida was to surpass the limits of the original colony many times over, as outlying districts sprang up all along the roads that led out of the town, next to the grounds of the local necropolis. These neighbourhoods, comprising as they did both dwellings and buildings dedicated to industry and interspersed with the said burial places, have been discovered –amongst other places– at the site of the Museum and in the vicinity of the *Casa del Mitreo.*

Certain details of the urban road network are known to us, although the reconstruction put forward at the beginning of the century cannot today be totally accepted. According to the map published at that time by the archaeologist Maximiliano Macías, a total of fourteen sewers were arranged perpendicular to the river, whilst a further nine ran parallel to the water flow. Only one –that which served the *kardo maximus*– flowed into the river Albarregas. The said drainage channels were built with great uniformity, and today their outlets can be clearly made out along the dam on the River Guadiana.

As far as one can tell, the layout of the streets of Mérida gave rise to a series of *insulae* or plots of land measuring 100-110 metres in length by 50-60 metres in width. Some such plots, however, in accordance with the streets that bounded them, were shorter in length and had an almost quadrangular design, measuring a mere 80 by 70-75 metres.

With regard to the urban area taken as a whole, we possess a lot of information on the design of several streets, in particular the main ones, namely the *decumanus* and the *kardo maximus*. These roads were paved with a bluish diorite stone extracted from nearby quarries and were lined –at least, that is , the main ones– by pavements and porticos reminiscent of the modern-day arcades.

19

As far as the public places of Roman Mérida are concerned, we have some knowledge as to the aspect of the town´s fora.

The forum that we consider to have been of a municipal nature, that is, the one intended for the use of the inhabitants themselves, featured the following elements: a temple, namely the *Templo de Diana;* a basilica, which was probably situated directly opposite the said place of worship; a square paved with limestone slabs; possibly some *thermae* or hot baths that would have been located near the *Calle Baños;* a curia or municipal senate whose precise location remains unknown; and also a portico, part of which was recently unearthed close to the point at which *Calle Sagasta* and *Calle San José* intersect.

Taking into consideration the remains that have come to light within the area of the forum, we can establish the limits of this most peculiar public space as being marked by the present-day *Calle de San José* and *Calle de Los Maestros,* on the one hand, and by the *Templo de Diana* and *Calle de Viñeros,* on the other.

We know that there was another such public place in Roman Mérida, but in this case the process of determining the exact shape it took has proven to be far more problematic. Could it have been the provincial forum of the colony, the one dedicated to the affairs of Lusitania, as we are led to deduce from certain dedications of a provincial nature made in worship of the Empire?

The most remarkable feature of this practically unknown architectural ensemble, apart from the above-mentioned *Arco de Trajano* (Trajan´s Arch), is a temple which, apparently devoted to imperial worship, was discovered in the course of recent excavations undertaken at the end of *Calle Holguin.* The temple comprised a high, concrete-structured *podium* or base which was faced by granite ashlars clad with slabs of marble. Marble was also the material employed for the various architectural elements of the temple, such as the enormous tambours which, measuring 1.5 m in diameter, give us some idea as to the monumental character of this building. It would seem that its portico took the form of a tetrastyle and, although we will only be fully sure after an in-depth study has been carried out, this could well be the temple that appears on the coins pertaining to the Roman colony, a temple dedicated to *Aeternitas Augusti,* an imperial virtue characteristic of provincial worship. The staircase that led up to the temple entrance began its ascent from the *Arco de Trajano* (Trajan´s Arch).

Another building belonging to Roman Mérida is known to us via an engraving by Alejandro de Laborde, although we cannot be sure as to its exact function. This building was situated a stone´s throw away from the above-mentioned temple, in Calle del Calvario.

Another clearly defined area of the colony´s urban fabric was that which held the buildings devoted to the performance of public spectacles, namely the Theatre and the Amphitheatre. The main axes of these most singular buildings were aligned with those of the town´s principal edifices, as a result of which it would

**16.** *Theatre. Scene façade.*

seem that they had been conceived right from the very beginning, a theory that is further corroborated by the records that perdure regarding the dates of their respective inaugurations.

**17. and 18.** *Theatre. Orchestra entrance. Vault.*

The Circus, originating as it did at a later date than the monuments we have just referred to, has a somewhat different history, its orientation having been determined in accordance with the course of the road leading from *Emerita* to *Corduba*.

Some examples of the houses that existed at the time of the Roman colony still survive, and we shall deal with them in due course.

The necropolises or cemeteries were arranged so as they encircled the town, lying just off the roads, in a manner reminiscent of a "funeral wreath". In the various areas where the existence of such cemeteries is to be made out, the tombs are seen to lie in perfect alignment, each necropolis thus being conferred an almost urban structure. These cemeteries contain a wide range of different types of sepulchres.

The most important burial sites are those to be found on the other side of the bridge that leads over the river Guadiana, where a number of quadrangular mausoleums dating from the 1st to 2nd centuries A.D. were unearthed, in the Albarregas valley and, in the vicinity of the Theatre, the so-called eastern necropolis, the limits of which reach out as far as the Circus and which can be regarded as being the most spectacular of the cemeteries owing to the structures

that have been preserved there.

Particularly noteworthy are the tombs belonging to the Julios and Voconios families, which are wrongly referred to as "Columbaria". These are open-air tombs inside which there are a number of recesses designed to hold the ashes of the dead. In the Voconios family mausoleum, there is an interesting series of portraits of the family members.

In the Visigothic era, the urban centre of Emerita did not undergo any far-reaching changes, although the aspect of the town´s public spaces was in fact considerably altered as a result of the erection of a series of new buildings. This development was to have an enormous effect on two districts in particular: on the one hand, the area comprising the present-day *Plaza de España*, where, on the site that is occupied today by the Church of *Santa María*, the *ecclesia senior* or old cathedral was to be found, and on the other, the area surrounding the Church of *Santa Eulalia*, where in the shadow of the basilica, whose original ground plan was recently discovered, a first-class religious complex was fashioned.

Moreover, several new districts were established on the outskirts of the town, their focal point being the said basilicas.

22

# BUILDINGS DEVOTED
# TO PUBLIC SPECTACLES:
# THE THEATRE, AMPHITHEATRE AND CIRCUS

## The Theatre

The Theatre is the most important monument from Roman times still surviving in Mérida. The Theatre and the Amphitheatre were jointly conceived by the Romans, the site chosen for their construction being a number of *insulae* or plots of land in the north-western corner of the town, at what was to turn out to be the highest point of the latter. In order to overcome the problem of the lashing winds –which doubtless would have bothered spectators and actors alike– the tiers of the auditorium were erected against the *San Albín* hillside.

These two buildings for the viewing of spectacles are separated –and at the same time united– by a Roman road, the very road that we shall take in order to start our tour of the monument. As we stroll along this road, we shall stop awhile to admire the solidity and robustness of the outer façade of the Theatre, a façade built using a rock-hard mortar of lime and stones and faced with well-squared granite ashlars featuring the characteristic rustication obtained by the chamfering of their arrises.

Access to the interior of the Theatre is gained by any one of 16 gates that are positioned along the façade. Preferably, however, we should make our entrance through the gates that lead us into the *media* section of the auditorium, where if we so wish we can take a short rest and, finding a comfortable spot, admire this most singular of monuments in all its grandeur and magnificence.

The tiered seating of the auditorium, which was reached by means of vaulted corridors *(vomitoria)*, was divided into three parts *(ima, media and summa cavea)* separated by wide passages *(praecinctiones)* and little walls *(baltei)* and indicative of the highly hierarchical structure of Roman society.

The most deteriorated part of the auditorium is its *summa cavea* or upper section. When the vaults of the corridors leading to the latter collapsed, it was split up

**19.** *Theatre. Peristyle.*

into seven great concrete projections. This event was to give rise to the legend of the "Seven Chairs" –the name by which this place is commonly known–, according to which seven Moorish kings are said to have sat on the said projections in order to decide on the fate that the town should suffer. This was the part of the auditorium reserved for slaves and the poorer classes of society.

The *media cavea,* which was made up of five rows of steps, was intended for the free plebeians.

The *ima cavea* or lower auditorium features 22 rows of steps that were set aside for the *equites* or cavalrymen, as is to be deduced from an inscription (EXD) which, engraved into one of the steps, has been interpreted as reading as follows: *"equites decem decreto (decurionum)",* in other words "room for ten cavalrymen by decree of the decurions". Thanks to this inscription, and on performing a simple rough calculation, it can be estimated that the theatre had a seated capacity of around 6,000 spectators.

The various tiers of the *cavea* or auditorium were interconnected by means of staircases which in turn divided the latter vertically into sections called *cunei.*

Only the highest strata of Roman society were allowed to witness a performance from the *orchestra,* a semicircular area paved with white and bluish-hued marbles and set aside for the chorus. Here, senators or high-ranking officials attending a performance would be given portable seats *(subsellia),* which were placed on three steps that were originally made of marble but which have been reconstructed in brick.

In order to gain access to the *orchestra* from the street, it was necessary to pass through vaulted corridors called *itinera* which came out in flat-arched openings bearing the following inscription: M.AGRIPPA.L.F.COS.III.TRIB.POT.III, that is to say, "Marcus Agrippa, son of Lucius, consul for the third time, exercising tribunal authority for the third time". By means of the references contained in the inscription we are informed as to the date of the inauguration of the Theatre, which occurred between the years 16 and 15 B.C. and possibly coincided with Emerita being conferred the status of provincial capital.

Situated at either end of the hemicycle, over the above-mentioned corridors, were tribunes of honour *(tribunalia),* reminiscent of the boxes at present-day theatres.

Between the orchestra and the stage *(pulpitum)* runs the interesting proscenium *(proscaenium),* a wall featuring alternating semicircular and rectangular bays in an attempt to improve –if this were possible– the already perfect acoustics of the theatre. On either side of the proscenium was a small flight of steps connecting it with the 60-metre long and 7-metre wide stage, along which the actors would parade. The stage floor, which was originally made of wood, was protected by a canopy that also acted as a sounding board.

The most outstanding element of the theatre is the scene façade *(scaenae frons),* featuring as it does three doorways –a large central one *(valva regia)* and two smaller side ones *(valvae hospitalia)*– through which the actors would enter stage. This magnificent "backcloth" consists of a 2.6-metre tall podium supporting two levels of Corinthian columns which, together with their respective entablatures, rise up to a height of almost 13 metres.

The intercolumniations, or the spaces between the columns, once housed a collection of statues portraying emperors in heroic postures, in military attire or even as deified figures, along with sculptures of gods from the classical Pantheon, such as Ceres, Pluto and Proserpine.

If we venture through any of the doorways of the scene façade, we will come across the *choragia,* or actors´ dressing rooms, the walls of which are lined with continuous benches covered in marble.

A common feature of most of the important Roman theatres such as this one at Mérida was a peristyle which, located at the back of the structure and surrounded by a colonnade, was the place where the spectators would stretch their legs in-between acts. The garden, whose appearance in Roman times cannot have been very different from that which it offers today, featured a canal by way of a pond and was profusely adorned with sculptures.

At the very heart of the peristyle, in line with the *valva regia* or central scene doorway, there is a small room floored with marble, in which in the course of archaeological excavations an important sculptural ensemble was discovered. Amongst the most noteworthy of the finds were the veiled head of Augustus portrayed as the High Priest, the effigies of Tiberius and Drusus, and a series of epigraphical records that duly reveal that this place was dedicated to the worship of the reigning emperor.

The Theatre underwent restoration from the years 333 to 335 A.D., a period which saw the introduction of new decorative architectural elements and the construction of a road encircling the entire monument.

Years later, when the theatre no longer fulfilled its original function, a private individual had the idea of erecting, right within the very grounds of the theatre,

**20. and 21.** *Theatre. Basilica house and sacred hall.*

**22.** *Amphitheatre. Panorama.*

his own house, the remains of which are partly still to be seen today. The most remarkable of the rooms of this house is one that features a double apse, a fact which led those involved in the excavations to believe that this was one of the places in Emerita where Christian worship was first performed and to dub the building *Casa-Basilica,* or House-Basilica, the name by which it is known in archaeological circles. What we are really faced with here, however, is a simple, typical domestic construction of the late Empire. The painted figures that appear on the walls, which at one time were identified as being Christian priests, are in fact representations of the servants that worked in the house, the latter having been a highly fashionable decorative theme in the late antiquity. Situated to the left of these noble quarters and the peristyle that lies before it one can see the private *thermae* that once belonged to the owner of the house.

In the course of the modern era, the Theatre became buried as a result of the deposition of earth on this site, and the land that overlay it was used for the cultivation of cereals and legumes. Such was its fate until the beginning of the present century, when, under the auspices of José Ramón Mélida and led by Mérida´s own Maximiliano Macías, archaeological excavations began. The 1960s witnessed the restoration of the Theatre to the aspect it affords today, a process carried out by the architect José Menéndez Pidal. Every year during the summer season a number of plays are performed at the Theatre.

The *cavea* or auditorium, which had a capacity of 15,000 spectators, was divided into three sections. The *ima cavea* or the section nearest to the arena featured a reserved row where special seats could be set out for the magistrates who presided the games. The *media cavea* and *summa cavea* accommodated people from a variety of classes and walks of life. The audience found their way to their seats by means of a series of staircases or *scalaria*.

The Roman Amphitheatre at Mérida is of

**23.** *Amphitheatre. Entrance gateway.*

### The Amphitheatre

The Amphitheatre was erected next to the Theatre, and, as was the case with the latter, the San Albín hillside was used as a support for its tiered auditorium. Two insulae or plots of land were set aside for its construction, and together the two monuments constituted what can be regarded as a fundamental part of the overall urban design of the *Emerita Augusta* colony.

considerable proportions. Its elliptical form measures just over 126 metres along its longest axis and has a width of 102 to 65 metres. According to the estimates of the director of the excavations, J.R. Mélida, the arena itself measures 54 metres by 41.15 metres.

The façade of the building is pierced here and there by a total of sixteen gateways, from which a series of *vomitoria* or entrance passages lead off into to the various sections of the auditorium.

At the Amphitheatre, just as was the case at the other buildings devoted to public spectacles, a special tribune was set aside for the highest dignitaries who came to preside the games in order that they might enjoy the performance in the greatest of comfort and be able to appreciate the games right down to the smallest of their details. Directly opposite this part of the auditorium, on the western side, stood another tribune, the *editoris tribunal*, reserved for the citizens who had financed the games.

Each of these *tribunalia* bore an identically-worded monumental inscription, which read: "The Emperor Augustus, son of the Divine Caesar, Supreme Pontifex, Consul for the eleventh time, Emperor for the fourteenth time". Engraved on long granite lintels, these honorific references clearly enlighten us as to the year –8 B.C.– in which the amphitheatre was inaugurated.

Subsequent to the archaeological research undertaken by Mélida, further inscriptions have come to light confirming the existence of two other tribunes which, situated on the northern and southern sides of

**24.** *Amphitheatre.*
*Western entrance.*

**25.** *Amphitheatre.*
*Reconstructed tribune.*

the auditorium, were similar in design to those of the amphitheatre at Verona.

The podium of the Amphitheatre was richly ornamented with large slabs of marble and featured an ashlar parapet decorated with paintings allusive to the games and contests that took place here. Some of these paintings are on display at the National Museum of Roman Art.

The gladiators would make their way down to the arena through two spacious corridors. Situated on either side of these were rooms whose ultimate purpose has yet to be determined. It has been suggested that they were possibly a place of worship dedicated to Nemesis, the guardian deity of the gladiators to whom the latter would commend themselves before going into the arena to face their fate. The theory has also been ventured that these rooms were provided for the exclusive use of the gladiators themselves. Both of the above explanations, however, are ruled out by the fact that the rooms are too small in size to be used for such ends. Indeed it would seem that the purpose of these rooms was rather that of housing the wild animals before the contests. This would explain the presence of a small elbow-shaped window through which the beasts could be safely fed.

26. *Candle-holder depicting a struggle between gladiators.*

27. *Amphitheatre. Painting portraying a wild animal fight.*

At the centre of the arena a large ditch or *fossa arenaria* was dug in the shape of a cross, the purpose of which was to store the stage machinery for the spectacle and the cages for the wild animals. This *fossa* was hidden from the view of the spectators by means of boarding supported by wooden posts. Later on in time, a layer of hydraulic mortar *(opus signinum)* was applied to the walls of the ditch, which was used as a water deposit.

Most of the gladiators who took part in the contests here were taken from the servile sectors of society, although there was no shortage of men prepared to fight for money (the *auctorati)*, as was the case with a number of veteran soldiers who were well versed in the use of weapons.

The physical condition of the gladiators varied immensely. The *noxi ad gladium ludi damnati* were men who had been condemned to die at spectacles such as these, and cannot really be regarded as true gladiators, since although they were allowed to brandish a weapon –a rule that was not always observed–, most of them had had no training whatsoever in either swordsmanship or the techniques of armed combat, and consequently it was practically a foregone conclusion that they would meet their death in the contest. It would seem that this was precisely what happened to the gladiator from Mérida *Cassius Victorinus,* who died at the age of 35 –a rather uncommon event for a gladiator– and who fought as a *retiarius,* that is, armed with a net and wielding a trident.

With a view to rendering the combat that much more attractive, when fighting amongst themselves, the gladiators would each use different arms and fighting techniques. In this way, the *retiarius* would have to measure up against the heavily armed *secutor.* Curiously enough, it is to the latter category that the only other gladiator known to have existed in Mérida belongs. *Sperchius* by name, he had been born in Frigia (Asia Minor) and was to meet his end at Emerita at the age of 24.

When a gladiator fought wild animals, he was referred to as a *venator.* Due to the fact that the entrepreneurs financing the contests were anxious to display exotic animals in their spectacles, it was not long before the trade in beasts from Asia and Africa flourished, real fortunes exchanging hands on occasions to secure the presence of certain species.

In all likelihood, the Amphitheatre at Mérida was abandoned in the early 5th century A.D., its fabric being used as a source of stone for the construction of new buildings. In modern times, even the *summa cavea* was demolished, pulled down using dynamite.

## The Circus

The site chosen for the construction of the Circus, situated 400 metres east of the colony´s perimeter wall, was an area of the valley floor near the *San Lázaro* aqueduct, a part of the town that was well served by one of the major Roman roads, that which united Emerita with *Corduba* (Córdoba) and *Toletum* (Toledo). In time, the northern façade of the Circus was to be erected parallel to the said road. The sheer enormity of the dimensions of the Circus (which measured over 30,000 square metres) constituted the only reason why it was not included in the district of the town devoted to public spectacles.

The passing of time has wrought havoc in the fabric of this renowned building, and nowadays it is practically impossible to imagine the aspect it afforded at the peak of its splendour. Nevertheless, it remains the best-preserved construction of its kind in the entire Iberian peninsula.

The series of excavations undertaken at the site of the Circus –which are still going on today– commenced way back in the year 1920. However, a number of questions concerning the building as yet remain unanswered. For instance, if we are to go by the knowledge that is currently held on the Circus, it is not possible to determine the date of its construction; in spite of this, it is generally thought that according to all logic it must have been built at the same time as the Theatre and the Amphitheatre, the dates of which have been firmly established as belonging to the reign of Augustus.

The shape of the Circus at Mérida is the characteristic one for this kind of monument, featuring two long straight parallel sections that are crowned in a semicircular fashion at one end and finished off with a slight curve at the other. It was in these two longer sides of the Circus that the tiered seating was installed. Whereas the southern side was built so as it rested on natural land forms, the northern flank had to be erected over a series of enormous concrete vaults. Up to the beginning of the last century the tiers of seats, whilst not remaining intact, were at least more complete than they are today. The French traveller Alejandro de Laborde, to whom we are greatly indebted for his excellent collection of engravings of Mérida, managed to count as many as eleven rows of seats. Nowadays one can only see the rows belonging to the sector nearest to the arena.

The auditorium was divided into a number of sections, or *caveas,* which could comfortably seat a total of 30,000 spectators. Seats enjoying the best views were reserved for the *editor* or the person

**28.** *Remains of the circus.*

financing the games and for the judges *(tribunal judicum)* who refereed the Circus events.

The *porta pompae,* the gateway from which the solemn cortège would begin its procession, was one of the most monumental in nature. Arranged along its façade were twelve *carceres* or chariot houses, each of which held one such vehicle. The *carceres* at the Mérida circus were formed by four pillars –one at each corner, the same as at the *Lepis Magna* circus– which in turn were surrounded by a wall whose outward-facing side may well have been decorated by columns or pilasters, as was the case in *Bovillae.* Once in the main passageway, which they entered via a large opening, the chariots would make their way along spacious corridors to take up the positions they had been allocated in a draw held previously. Then, when the referee presiding over the races waved a white standard or *mappa,* the gates of the chariot houses would be raised, thus letting the chariots out into the arena, where the races themselves would take place. The arena at the Mérida circus was truly spectacular, measuring as it did over 400 metres by nearly 96, as a result of which it ranked as one of the

biggest of its day. A 233-metre long wall running longitudinally across the arena divided the latter into two in the manner of a backbone, whence it received its name, *spina.* All that remains of the *spina* of the circus of Emerita Augusta are its concrete foundations, although, as was the case at other circuses, it must at one time have been adorned with statues and obelisks, traces of which are still to be seen. At either end of the *spina* stood the finishing posts or *metae* marking the point at which the chariots had to turn.

The chariots could either be drawn by two horses *(bigae)* or by four *(quadrigae)* and were driven by *aurigas,* charioteers who were divided up into a number of teams or *factiones* each identified by a colour, namely the greens, the whites, the reds and the blues. Various sources inform us as to some of the charioteers who scaled the heights of fame at the Mérida circus. This is where the Lusitanian Cayo Apuleyo Diocles, the most famous *agitador* or chariot driver of all time, is supposed to have begun his long sporting career. After winning a total of 1,462 races, he retired at the age of 42, by which time he had amassed a considerable personal fortune.

**29.** *Mosaic featuring circus motifs (4th century A.D.).*

A section of flooring dating from the second half of the 4th century A.D. that was discovered in Mérida and is now kept at the Museum supplies us with a wealth of information as to the attire worn by the *aurigas.* It features portrayals of two such charioteers, namely *Marcianus* and *Paulus,* the former also being celebrated in a mosaic from the Roman town of Italica. The charioteers sported corsets with leather straps and a thick belt onto which their reins would be fastened and carried a small knife in order to cut themselves free from the reins if need be, and thus avoid being dragged around the arena in the event that the chariot overturned. This was no strange sight at the Circus, particularly if we bear in mind that the chariots themselves, as is the case of the one depicted in the mosaic, were almost entirely made of wicker. Completing the charioteers´ attire was a metal helmet that protected their heads and a whip with which they would drive on their team of horses.

The circus at *Emerita* underwent restoration during the 4th century A.D. This fact has come to our knowledge thanks to an inscription made on marble that was originally placed in the vicinity of the *carceres,* where it was found, and which today is kept at the National Museum of Roman Art. Engraved in the period from October 337 to March-April 340, the inscription reads thus: "In this most happy and prosperous century, rendered so by the good fortunes and the clemency of our illustrious, brave and all-conquering lords and emperors Flavius Claudius Constantinus and Flavius Julius Constantius, the most distinguished count Tiberius Flavius Letus ordered that the circus, which was crumbling with age, be reconstructed, fitted out with new ornamentation, and flooded with water. This task having been taken on by the most excellent Julius Saturninus, governor of the province of Lusitania, the suitably restored appearance of the circus was to provide the magnificent colony of Emerita the greatest possible pleasure".

The most striking feature of the entire inscription is the reference to the intentional flooding of the circus with water. Some modern-day authorities on the subject believe that the circus was thus transformed into a *naumanchia,* that is, a stage on which naval battles could be simulated. Such a hypothesis, however, would seem to be highly unlikely due to the enormous dimensions of the circus. The idea that only certain parts of the arena were flooded, thus creating a series of ponds, gives rise to reservations as to whether such an undertaking would have been technically possible at that time. The wording of this part of the inscription could merely refer to the installation of fountains in the arena; its true meaning, however, remains a mystery.

It should be pointed out that the reconstruction of the circus took place at a very late date, a fact which clearly demonstrates the great passion displayed by the people of Emerita towards this type of spectacle. Neither should it be forgotten that just a few years prior to the reconstruction of this monument, the Fathers of the Church, who had gathered at the First Council of Elvira (310 A.D.), pronounced an anathema or ban on circus games which they deemed to be shameful in nature. Four years later, the First Council of Arles condemned the *aurigas* and warned them to give up their profession, threatening them with excommunication if they were to disobey. It is important that we bring such information to light, since the fact remains that the circus at Emerita continued to play host to chariot races until at least the 6th century. This we know thanks to an interesting inscription that was discovered at the spot referred to as *Casa Herrera,* which we will deal with more exhaustively later on in the book. The inscription in question is that appearing on the tombstone of a certain charioteer called Sabinianus, who lived to the age of around 46. From the tombstone it is to be deduced that Sabinianus was both an *auriga* and a Christian and that he was buried as such, without having to relinquish a profession that must have brought him the attention of numerous enthusiastic admirers as well as considerable financial rewards. The inscription on Sabinianus´ tombstone was made at least 50 years subsequent to the Council of Elvira. Moreover, if we are to take into account the fact that Bishop Liberius of Mérida was in attendance at the said council, it will become apparent that the wishes of the Church and those of some of its faithful did not always go hand in hand. Once chariot races had finally been outlawed, however, the circus entered upon a slow process of decline which was not to be reversed until the present-day, when efforts are finally being made to restore its former glory.

## THE NATIONAL MUSEUM OF ROMAN ART

In commemoration of the bimillenary of the town of Mérida in 1975, the Spanish government decided to create a National Museum of Roman Art to replace the old Roman Museum that had been founded by royal decree on the 26th March 1838. It was furthermore determined that a new building should be erected on the site called *Las Torres* to house and display the rich variety of Roman remains that had been found in Mérida. The sheer importance of the said remains was to explain why the new museum was to be considered an institution of national relevance.

The new museum was opened on 19th September 1986 by Their Majesties the King and Queen of Spain, in the presence of the President of the Italian Republic.

Having been entrusted with the task of planning the museum building, the prestigious architect Rafael Moneo Vallés proceeded to conceive a magnificent opus that has been rightly acclaimed by all who have had the opportunity of seeing it and which constitutes a new departure in the whole concept of Spanish museums. As was clearly the effect sought after by the museum´s creator, the building contains a number of elements reminiscent of Roman architecture. This is to be seen above all in the layout of the crypt, as well as in the main hall and on the façades.

Occupying a plot of land measuring almost 4,500 square metres, the building is situated directly opposite the Theatre-Amphitheatre complex, to which it is joined by means of a long tunnel. The entire construction is made up of a concrete core clad with brick facings.

**30.** *Roman Museum. Glass case holding pottery.*

33

**31.** *View of the main hall of the Museum.*

The western façade, which runs along *Calle José Ramón Mélida,* is of a hard and robust nature and calls to mind certain buildings of the Late Empire. Here, we find the main entrance, featuring as it does a marble lintel that is inscribed with the word MUSEO and above which there is a niche that is intended to house a sculpture of large proportions. The doorway comprises two leaves, on which the designs of the most noteworthy of Mérida´s monuments are represented in bas-relief.

Architecturally speaking, the southern façade of the museum, in keeping with the administrative nature of the section of the building it encloses, has a rather more domestic appearance.

On contemplating the eastern façade, which features a number of outstanding traits, one can discern certain parts of the internal structure of the building which are otherwise practically impossible to imagine from the outside. Finally, the northern face of the museum, whilst extremely simple in design, includes exaggerated openings that break up the monotonous character imposed by the enormity of the massive side structure.

The museum building is seen to be divided into two basic parts, one of which is devoted entirely to exhibition purposes, whereas the other is reserved for the museum administration and for the provision of other facilities. The two sections are united by a gallery hanging over a Roman road.

Once inside the building, the visitor is led on via a ramp into the main hall of the Museum. Boasting enormous dimensions, the hall comprises a succession of nine identical arches, the shape of which is similar to that of the *Arco de Trajano* (Trajan´s Arch), itself one of the most extraordinary monuments of Mérida. The said arches serve to support the roof structure, which in turn provides a series of large skylights intended to make use of the daylight. Thus, natural light cascades down, flooding every nook and cranny of the exhibition area.

**32.** *Genius of the Colony (2nd century A.D.).*

**33.** *Mithraic sculpture (2nd century A.D.).*

**34.** *Group of sculptures portraying the imperial family, pertaining to the sacred hall of the Theatre.*

**35.** *Bust of Augustus.*

**36.** *Funeral monument to the memory of Zósimo (3rd century A.D.).*

Apart from its central space, the main hall has two clearly differentiated sections. Firstly, on the left, there is an area whose size and structure are ideal for the positioning of large sculptures; and secondly, on the right, we find a space that takes the shape of a second, transversal hall and in which the various objects are displayed in an axial fashion, either placed on pedestals or hanging from the walls. The back end of each of the said sections –featuring arches whose rise is larger than that of a semicircular arch– is divided up into a series of recesses which give out onto a corridor that can barely be made out from a distance. Providing the perfect place for the display of important items, these recesses have a certain power of attraction that invites the visitors to go and take a closer look.

In each and every one of the exhibition areas afforded by the Museum on Its three constituent levels, essentially educational criteria have been followed in the attempt to reflect, in the form of highly expressive archaeological objects, the different aspects of the day-to-day existence of that great town of the Western Roman Empire, *Emerita Augusta*.

The larger-sized remains have been well set out and are to be seen either standing on a series of granite pedestals or hanging from the museum walls. All smaller items are housed in the respective glass cabinets.

The said display cabinets were designed exclusively for the museum and comprise a brass framework supporting panes of armoured glass, the whole structure being backed by a stuccoed surface which is either Pompeian red or white in colour, depending on the particular exhibits to be displayed. The free-standing cabinets on the ground floor also feature a marble socle and a wooden base and are structured in such a way that it is possible for a person to actually enter the cabinet in order to clean it. Besides these cabinets the museum also contains other types of recipients and show cases in the shape of counters with wooden pedestals for the display of, amongst other things, candle-holders, bones and various items fashioned in gold and silver.

The information provided for the visitors to the museum is of a simple, direct nature. A general description as to the contents of each room is given on large panels, whilst a brief identification of the individual items is supplied on a series of small signs.

We shall now proceed to give details as to the different rooms that go to make up the museum, highlighting the various sections they comprise and their general appearance.

**37.** *Mosaic depicting the rape of Europe (3rd century A.D.).*

### Ground Floor

The first three exhibition areas or rooms to be seen on the ground floor of the museum are devoted to the buildings that were the scene for spectacles, namely the Theatre, the Amphitheatre and the Circus.

The rooms lying on the left, taking the form of large cells or recesses, house a collection of monumental statues that were discovered in the course of the excavations undertaken at the Theatre. The statues are spread out around a space featuring three sections united by a series of beautiful arches, as a result of which the exhibits can be observed from a variety of different perspectives. Particularly noteworthy amongst

In Room II an attempt has been made to symbolically reconstruct the central axis of the Theatre, highlighting the political and religious purpose of the latter. The impressive gallery of imperial portraits depicting Augustus, Agrippina, Drusus and Tiberius, along with the altar stone and pedestals unearthed at the Theatre, provide ample evidence of both the religious and propagandistic rôle played by the Theatre.

Finally, in Room III the visitor is informed as to the physical evolution of this outstanding monument of Roman Mérida. The most significant restorations it has undergone are documented by the architectural elements on show and the inscriptions that bear witness to the latter.

**38.** *Reconstruction of a room featuring paintings from the 4th century A.D.*

the items on display here are the statue of Pluto, the effigy of Ceres that overlooks the group of sculptures from up on its high pedestal, and the representations of emperors in military attire.

Situated on the right-hand side of this floor in the transversal hall, Room I contains a display of objects related to the Amphitheatre and the Circus, such as memorial stones commemorating the inauguration of the Amphitheatre (in the year 8 B.C.), a reconstruction of the Amphitheatre balustrade complete with paintings alluding to the games that took place in the arena, and a commemorative tablet recalling the restoration of the Circus in the period from 337 to 340 A.D.

Rooms IV and V are dedicated to the religions of *Emerita Augusta*. The town acted as a veritable magnet for many groups of citizens who came here from all over the Empire, a fact which would explain the variety of different forms of worship that were developed in the colony. Thus the people of Mérida took part in the official State cults, the veneration of the deities of the classical pantheon, the worship of eastern gods and the truly indigenous religions. Particularly noteworthy here are the sculptures and inscriptions that were found in the area of the sanctuary of Mithras. The zenith of Mithraism is said to have been reached in the second half of the 2nd

**39. and 40.** *Group of sculptures from the Forum Portico (1st Century A.D.) and a close-up of one of the figures.*

**41.** *Nilotic mosaic (2nd century A.D.).*

**42.** *Mosaic featuring a hunting scene (4th century A.D.).*

**43.** *Mosaic by Annius Bonus (4th century A.D.).*

century A.D., a period in which the powerful figure of the great priest *Gaius Accius Hedychrus* acted as a leading light. Amongst the other riches on display here are the magnificent mosaic crafted by *Annius Bonus* on the theme of Bacchus and Ariadne, the effigy of the patron of Roman Mérida –the so-called *Genius Coloniae–*, together with another image which, having been discovered at recent excavations, seemingly represents a mythical figure. This fine collection is added to and further embellished by several inscriptions alluding to divinities, an example of

Emerita´s dead, the presence of a *cuppa* and the sepulchre of Zósimo, the intendant of the VII Legion, featuring a stepped base.

As yet unfinished in the museum is the installation of the collection of remains that illustrate the aspect afforded by Roman houses in Mérida. At present there is in particular one mosaic on display –that depicting the Rape of Europe– which can be considered a fine example of the quality of mosaic floorings that prevailed in the houses of the colony. The most outstanding feature of this section, however, is the

**44 and 45.** *Male and female representations dating from the 1st century A.D.*

which is the one that refers to Proserpine, the deity after whom the town reservoir was named, and which occupies a commanding position over the glass display cabinets of Room V

Meanwhile, Room VI deals with the subject of funeral rites in Roman Mérida. The excavations carried out in the grounds of the cemeteries that once surrounded the town have unearthed a number of items, as a result of which the museum is able to display a wide variety of types of interment used for both buried and cremated remains. We should perhaps highlight, amongst the large number of tombstones, altars, memorial pillars and stelae that reveal the identity and circumstances of several of

reconstruction of the pictorial decoration that once adorned a Roman house. The paintings belong to a specific genre and are the work of a fine artisan who, clearly endowed with a certain skill for drawing, knew just how to satisfy the artistic tastes of his clientèle, capturing the scenes that were most in vogue at the time –the 4th century A.D.–, namely those depicting circus games and hunting feats. This particular group of exhibits is completed by a further two mosaic floors, on this occasion from the villa called *Las Tiendas* that was situated within the jurisdiction of Emerita. One of the mosaics is decorated by means of a number of large recipients, whilst the other portrays an interesting hunting episode in which a cavalryman is seen stalking a panther. Finally, the visitor comes to Rooms VIII, IX and X, the last on this floor of the museum, which have been conceived as a representation of public life in the forum of Emerita Augusta. Recent excavations performed in the grounds of the so-called "Temple of Diana" and in the adjoining portico have brought to light a number of important structures which bring us closer to a full understanding of the nature of the forum, a public space that was open to all citizens of Mérida.

The outstanding feature of the forum was the said monumental portico, itself the origin of the statues of togaed personalities on display in this part of the museum. It is known that at least the bodies of these statues were the work of the local sculptor *Gaius Aulus,* whose quality as an artist is clear for all to see. Belonging to the same sculptural ensemble were medallions depicting Jupiter, Amun and Medusa, which, together with the caryatids that flanked them, adorned the attic crowning the portico. Positioned as they are at the back of the great hall, these extraordinary exhibits are truly spectacular in appearance and possibly afford what can be considered the most memorable moment of any visit to the museum. Thanks to a collection of fragments pertaining to the said medallions which is on display in Room VIII, the public is able to admire in perfect detail the way in which these pieces were originally executed. The exhibition of items related to the forum of Emerita is rounded off by a number of capitals, a variety of different architectural elements and an enormous statue clad in military dress.

### Middle Floor

Upon entering the semi-darkness that pervades this part of the museum, which is likewise divided into a number of rooms –in this case nine–, one comes across two lines of wall display-cabinets and a series of show cases comprising various trays, all of which contain small items belonging to one or other of the industrial arts that are known to have existed in *Emerita Augusta.* An exhaustive selection of pottery and glass items, pieces crafted in bone and also a modest but significant collection of objects made in precious metal and coins is on display, accompanied in each case by the relevant explanatory information.

The glass collections to be seen in the museum are truly impressive, encompassing as they do a wide range of different items whose respective dates cover an extensive time span. The exhibits can be classified as belonging to one of two categories, namely glass

products of genuinely local origin or well-documented imported articles. Without wishing to overlook the other items on display on this floor, we should perhaps highlight the section dedicated to objects fashioned from bone, due to the great variety of forms and tools it contains.

As far as the coin collection is concerned –in spite of the fact that numismatic finds are not exactly over-represented in the museum– we would like to call the visitor´s attention to the pieces struck at the mint in *Emerita,* there being numerous examples on show of all the different types of coins ever issued here.

Of equal interest is the more or less accurate reconstruction of a *columbarium,* which includes the urns that were used to hold the ashes of the dead.

On this floor a wealth of information is made available to the public as regards the exact classification and purpose of each of the objects exhibited, along with details concerning the manufacture and commercial distribution of the same.

### Upper Floor

The upper floor of the museum is ideal for the viewing of further collections of objects that comprise, within their own particular context, memorial stones, sculptures and above all mosaics. Although the latter can in fact be examined from both the lower and middle levels of the museum, it is at this height that they can be best appreciated.

The magnificent light pouring down from the zenith considerably enhances the effect of sculptured items, such as the series of portraits crafted by the *Emerita* school or the inscriptions engraved on commemorative stones, altars and memorial pillars.

Taken as a whole, this last floor of the museum serves to show certain other aspects of Roman life in *Emerita Augusta,* an understanding of which is facilitated by the information provided.

Room I houses an exhibition of documents – mostly of an epigraphical nature– which refer to public posts in both the provincial and local administration. A small section of this room explains the way in which a water supply was provided for *Emerita Augusta,* and here we even come across the name of one of the conduits involved, namely *Aqua Augusta.*

The visual effect of the spectacular mosaic from the villa called *Las Tiendas,* featuring the scene of a wild boar-hunt and busts representing the Four Seasons, creates a fitting atmosphere for this first room on the upper floor.

The purpose of the next section is to illustrate a fact known by few and which could indeed come as a surprise to more than one visitor to the museum, namely the true extent of the territory belonging to the colony of *Emerita Augusta*. The limits of this territorial unit are set out in a diagram, whilst a variety of archaeological documents unearthed during the excavation of several *villae* help to explain the situation that prevailed in Roman times.

In the following two rooms (nos. III and IV), an analysis is made of *Emerita society*. The first of these rooms reviews the origin of the people who came to settle here, which, as the visitor will see, was extremely varied. The next room is concerned with the different occupations performed by the people of *Emerita*. In this respect the written sources have been far from sparse, and consequently we have come to learn the name of one or other famous *emeritense* such as the poet Decianus, a prestigious lawyer in Rome itself. However, we owe the great majority of such information to the inscriptions and objects that have been recovered by means of the excavation of the town´s ancient necropolises.

**47.** *Tree pictured in a relief dating from the 1st century A.D.*

**46.** *Mosaic representing the seven wise men (4th century A.D.).*

Amongst the most significant professions and trades known to have existed in Emerita are those of doctor, baker, potter, glassmaker, ceramist, sculptor and artist.

Possibly ranking as one of the most outstanding collections to be seen in the museum is that devoted to sculptured portraits, those unequalled works of the Emerita school. The information we have on the sculptors who worked in Roman Mérida provides a good illustration of the circumstances surrounding a highly active artistic community in a provincial town such as this. We have already mentioned *Gaius Aulus,* author of the officially commissioned statues gracing the forum, and to his name we should add a long list of artists, including Demetrios and other anonymous sculptors, who were capable of giving full expression to the art of portrait sculpting, an art characterized by a genuine realism and the suggestion of an attempt to get inside the mind of the person being depicted.

In Rooms V and VI the visitor can admire the most significant examples of this art form, the beauty of which is further enhanced by the abundant natural light that literally floods the rooms, revealing even the most minute detail of the figures on display.

**48.** *Stele dedicated to Lutatia (2nd century A.D.).*

Of course the museum would not be complete without a reference to the intellectual activity of *Emerita Augusta,* evidence of which is to be detected throughout the entire history of the Empire, although the clearest picture obtained in this area is perhaps that pertaining to the 4th century A.D. Bearing witness to the intellectual capacity of the most select inhabitants of the town are the following objects: the representation of a Muse, a somewhat crude creation not however totally devoid of grace; the Mosaic of the Seven Wise Men; the stele –of undoubted iconographical interest– crafted in the memory of the girl called *Lutatia Lupata,* along with various inscriptions composed in verse.

Finally we come to Room VIII which, dedicated to Paleo-Christian and Visigothic Mérida, constitutes the link between this institution and the planned future Museum of Visigothic Art and Culture that Mérida needs in order to display the wealth of archaeological remains dating from the said period. As a result of the importance gained by Emerita in its rôle as episcopal see as from the early 6th century, and being as it was under the protection of its strong-willed bishops, the town was to become the focal point for the development of Hispanic art in Visigothic times.

Lying beneath the whole exhibition area of the museum is a crypt which, somewhat reminiscent of a

Roman cryptoporticus, houses ruins that were recovered during the excavation of the museum site in preparation for the construction of the latter. Apart from the Roman road we have referred to above and a large section of the *San Lázaro* aqueduct, which were also brought to light on that occasion, the remains found on this site and preserved in the crypt belonged to a suburban district of Emerita situated near to the town walls and comprising both residential areas and burial grounds.

Constituting the highlight of the crypt are the ruins of a house featuring a porticoed courtyard and well-defined corridors. The rooms of the dwelling are decorated with paintings, one of which reveals two perfectly differentiated phases, one superimposed over the other. Completing the remains of the house is a second courtyard lined with a series of columns.

A further two rooms are partially preserved in the south-eastern corner of this extraordinary mine of archaeological treasures. The most remarkable aspect of this section is the room whose entrance is framed by columns and whose walls are decorated with paintings.

With regard to the burial grounds that once lay on this site, several tombs were found dating from a period spanning the 1st and the 3rd centuries A.D. The most important feature of the collection of funeral monuments held in the crypt is a mausoleum containing six juxtaposed tombs.

The impressive architecture on display in the crypt –an area in which the original levels of the archaeological finds have been respected– combined with the subdued light with which it is illuminated, renders any visit to this significant ensemble of ruins a most evocative experience.

**49.** *View of the crypt.*

The various floors that go to make up the other part of the museum complex are devoted to all aspects of administration and to the technical facilities of the museum, containing amongst other things a series of workshops, a library and an assembly hall.

THE SANTA EULALIA MONUMENT

One of the monuments that is most often overlooked by the majority of visitors to Mérida is the one that was erected in commemoration of the town´s patron saint and whose structure comprises a variety of different materials, notably certain Roman architectural elements.

The earliest record we have of the existence of this monument, as is the case with so many other of Mérida´s constructions, is that supplied by the town chronicler Bernabé Moreno de Vargas in the year 1633, the date of the first edition of his work entitled *History of the Town of Mérida,* since in this book he alludes to the presence of a statue and a number of column sections in the field of San Juan, ready to be

**50 and 51.** *The Santa Eulalia Obelisk, pictured in an old engraving and as it is today.*

converted into a magnificent obelisk. The origin of the said pieces of columns in unknown. Moreno suggests that the *aras* or altar stones came from the atrium of the so-called Temple of Diana, but there is nothing to confirm this. Furthermore, it is difficult to imagine just how the monument came to be set up in such a remote area of the town. The Field of San Juan or of Arrabal, as it was also known, was in Moreno´s days nothing more than an area of wasteland. What is certain is that some time must have passed before the idea for the intended construction actually began to take shape.

It was to be the appearance of a votive altar stone of red-veined white marble bearing a reference to the Concord of Augustus that would finally lend new force to the idea –which in the meantime had been abandoned– of raising a monument in honour of Mérida´s most revered virgin. The local authorities decided to place the stone in a public place so that in this way it would be known to everyone. It is to be imagined that the discovery of the altar stone caused something of a stir in the quiet Mérida of the 1600s, and even more so when it became known that certain inhabitants of the town had stolen the stone and taken it home with them. Moreno de Vargas´ very own son was to be the person who with great endeavour set about ensuring the stone´s recovery. It was at this point in time that it was considered not only opportune but also highly advisable that the stone, together with other highly valuable objects crafted in ancient times, "should form part of a pyramid" – according to the contemporary description recorded in the Municipal Historical Archive– that would be erected over a series of steps and which would feature at its apex "the image of St Eulalie".

This opus was begun –under the auspices of the town authorities– with the construction of a tiered pedestal consisting of five steps. Placed on top of this, acting as the plinth for the column, was the stone with the reference to the Concord of Augustus, which itself supported three cylindrical altar stones, two of which were beautifully adorned with bucrania (the skulls of sacrificed oxen), garlands and instruments of Roman liturgy. Then came a capital, followed by a block of stone featuring three coats of arms –those of Spain, Mérida and the town governor– and a cartouche, the latter bearing the following inscription: "This triumphal column was erected by the town of Mérida in honour of its patron saint Eulalie, under the governorship of field marshal Lope de Tordoya y Figueroa, knight of the Order of St James, in the year MDCLII". Crowning the whole structure was the image of the martyr St Eulalie, a gilded sculpture

crafted in white marble. However, the people of Mérida were only able to enjoy their new monument for a short time, since the weak points in its construction soon became manifest, as a result of which it had to undergo restoration in 1661.

In the late 19th century, at a time when Pedro María Plano was the man in charge of the town´s affairs, it was agreed to restore the damaged parts of the obelisk with marble mortar and at the same time to re-locate the monument at a site 40 metres upstreet from its original position. The tiered pedestal was replaced by a stone base, the corners of which were embellished with feigned half Tuscan columns, whilst each of its sides was adorned with rudimentary garlands that were in keeping with the decorative work to be seen on some of the noble stones it supported.

At the present moment in time, due to the fact that its surrounding area is undergoing a process of urban re-development, the obelisk has been dismantled and its constituent Roman parts transferred to the National Museum of Roman Art, where they are on display. It is planned to make replicas of the said components and to re-erect the monument, complete with the rest of its parts, in the avenue called *Rambla de la Mártir Santa Eulalia*.

**52.** *Temple of Mars. Detail of the frieze.*

## TEMPLE OF MARS

Leaving the *Santa Eulalia* obelisk behind us and carrying on for about 200 metres, we will come face to face with the remains of the Temple of Mars, situated next to the old Madrid road and in front of the Church of *Santa Eulalia* (see page 82).

Truth to be told absolutely nothing is known regarding the original structure of this building. Neither do we possess any information on its original location, since what has been preserved of its fabric

**53.** *Hornito de Santa Eulalia (Little oven of St Eulalie) and the remains of the Temple of Mars.*

are some remains that were re-used in the construction of a portico erected in Mérida in the course of the 17th century in front of a chapel that supposedly marked the site where the remains of the martyrized saint were buried during the reign of Emperor Diocletian. Unfortunately, very little contemporary information as to the origin of the remains has survived, however, an inscription in the left-hand corner of the temple´s architrave reads thus: "These carved stones of marble were found amongst the ruins of the town". The following are the surviving original elements of what was a truly extraordinary edifice: two fragments of marble columns of varying diameters and, resting on the latter, two Corinthian capitals, likewise fashioned in marble, together with six pieces of architrave, one of which, formerly used as a step, is now to be seen in the museum, and finally a cornice. The rest of the elements are imitations that were added when the building as we now it today was constructed in the 17th century.

Owing to their great artistic value, the pieces of architrave are by far the most outstanding elements of the temple, faced as they are by a frieze decorated with a combination of medallions containing medusa heads and both floral elements and palm leaf motifs. On the lower section of the architrave, seemingly vying for space, a whole range of items pertaining to both the attire and the armour of the Roman army are depicted, such as decorated shields, different types of weapons, chariot wheels, warrior attributes and military emblems. Placed at the centre of all these items is a series of medallions featuring trophies of war.

Appearing at the centre of the frieze, breaking up the line of ornamentation, is an inscription that informs us of the dedication of the temple to Mars, a ceremony performed by Vettilla, the wife of Paculus (MARTI SACRUM VETTILLA PACULI). This event possibly took place during the reign of the Antonines, since at that time Paculus, a member of the Roscios, a noble senatorial family, was in all likelihood the governor of Lusitania and therefore resident in Mérida. Further down on the frieze there is another inscription, on this occasion dating from modern times, which, likewise engraved in Latin, reminds us that the building is now no longer dedicated to Mars, but rather to Jesus Christ and to the martyr saint Eulalie. Crowning the structure is yet another inscription, in this case in Spanish, which recalls that in the year 1612, under the governorship of Luis Manrique de Lara, the town of Mérida rebuilt –with the aid of charitable donations– this chapel called the *Hornito de Santa Eulalia* (Little oven of St Eulalie), a name by which it is still known today.

## THERMAE BUILDING IN CALLE REYES HUERTAS

Originally sited in a district lying outside the town walls, surrounded by an extensive necropolis and almost next door to the House of the Amphitheatre, the building believed to have housed the *thermae* or Roman baths was first excavated in 1927 by José Ramón Mélida. Subsequently it was to fade into oblivion until a new excavation campaign was carried out in 1981, as a result of which this monumental building took on the appearance it has retained to the present day.

The remains, half of which still lie buried under the neighbouring houses, in their day constituted a building either of the *thermae* type or of an industrial nature. Nevertheless, owing to its situation in the vicinity of the Christian burial grounds adjacent to the basilica of *Santa Eulalia*, ever since ancient times scholars have sought to link the building with the primitive forms –whether they be orthodox or heretical– of Christian worship, or even to connect it with the cult of Mithras.

What can be seen today of the building is an architectural ensemble which, on its lowest level, comprises three large sections of concrete foundations. The first of these is quadrangular in form and has an eight-stepped staircase leading down it. It is connected via a small door to another octagonal section and is linked to a third one by means of a 13-metre long underground passage. This third section, the most interesting of the three, is a rotunda measuring 7.2 metres in diameter; all that remains of its vaulting is a single circular projection, at the centre of which eight circular granite pillars are preserved, arranged in a circle around a rubblework parapet of which today practically nothing remains. Leading off from this section to the north-west is another passageway, similar to the one mentioned above, which after 2 metres ends up in a wall containing a niche. A third passageway, situated directly opposite the first one, leads to a room measuring 4 by 5 square metres which is closed off to the east in the manner of an apse and opens out on its western side into a passage that slopes evenly down into a well 2.5 metres in diameter and 8 metres deep. The entire room is covered by continuous semicircular arches and ventilation is achieved by means of three chimneys. As far as the decoration of the room is concerned, its stuccowork sections are today barely visible. On the upper level of the building, positioned around the rotunda and even breaking through part of the original structure, it is still possible to make out the remains of hot water baths, with their respective *hypocausta*. This leads us to believe that, even if the building was not originally designed for use as hot baths or *thermae*, since it was probably first built for industrial purposes, with the passing of time it did in fact become adapted for such an end, a conversion which possibly took place in the late 3rd century or in the early 4th century A.D.

## FORUM PORTICO

In the area adjacent to the Temple of Diana there once existed a monumental portico which today has been partially reconstructed, together with the building of which it once formed part.

The existence of the portico came to light as early as the latter part of last century, when an authoritative member of the Subcommission for the Monuments of Mérida, Pedro María Plano, identified it as belonging to a hypothetical "Palace of the Praetors". At that time a series of decorative architectural elements had appeared, namely two togaed figures created by the sculptor *Gaius Aulus,* and another statue which has the name Agrippa written on its basis.

However, it was not to be until the present century, to be precise in the 1980s, that the number of finds on this site would multiply, thanks to the excavations carried out by the archaeologists of the national Museum of Roman Art, thus enabling the true worth of the remains discovered to be fully appreciated.

The portico once encircled a garden which in turn contained a channel lined with hydraulic mortar and clad in marble plates. The function of this channel was to drain off the water that fell from the roof covering a passageway or *ambulacrum* along which the contemporary *emeritenses* would often be seen out for a stroll. Other features of the portico were an inner wall pierced with a series of niches housing sculptures of both royal and mythological figures, and lastly an outer façade whose frieze bore a succession of medallions or *clypea* depicting Jupiter, Amun and Medusa –symbols representing the supreme power of Rome– and a number of caryatids, that is, female figures dressed in the classic Greek peplos, which in the manner of metopes lent the said medallions a highly individual aspect.

The portico of the municipal forum at Mérida was conceived in the 1st century A.D. as part of the second phase of work aimed at conferring this public space a more noble appearance, a process which involved the use of marble in the construction of buildings in place of granite, the material which had resorted to up to that point in time.

**54.** *Forum Portico. View of the reconstruction.*

50

**55.** *Trajan´s Arch.*

TRAJAN´S ARCH

Rising up majestically amidst the surrounding entangled labyrinth of modern constructions, masked by the houses lying adjacent to it, is the *Arco de Trajano,* or Trajan´s Arch, the monument that in ages past most aroused the admiration of travellers and historians.

The name given to the arch is a completely arbitrary one and is only to be explained as a product of popular fancy.

The truth is we have no knowledge as to the precise emperor under whose rule the arch was erected. Nevertheless, judging by the construction technique employed, we can safely say that what we have before us here is a typical example of Augustan architecture.

Built entirely in granite, the arch boasts an enviable robustness. A total of 23 voussoirs are seen to spring from its sturdy uprights. It is 13.79 metres high and 5.70 metres deep, whilst its span has been measured at 8.67 metres.

In ancient times the physical appearance of the arch must have been very different from the one it affords today. On either side of the central opening there would have been another two openings of considerably smaller dimensions. The holes appearing on some of the ashlars that go to make up the arch reveal that it was originally faced in marble, although it must also be said that many of the said orifices are simply holes where the heavy stone blocks were gripped by hooks so that they could be lifted into place.

Since the time in the 18th century when Villena Mosiño led an excavation at this site and mapped out the ground plan and the elevation of the arch, the belief has been held that one of the main arteries of Mérida, namely the *kardo maximus,* that which ran

51

across the north of the town, actually passed through the arch. We do not know whether the intention of this archaeologist was to offer a free interpretation of what he had seen or whether his conclusions were simply wrong, but the truth is that no such road has been found to pass under the arch, which instead would seem to have been graced by beautiful marble paving and the foot of a monumental staircase which would have led to the entrance of the temple recently discovered in *Calle Holguín.*

Bearing all this in mind, it would seem that the arch formed part of the urban layout of the town in the

*quadrata* or a basic foundational enclosure, the design of which would have been in line with the pattern established for Roman military camps. According to this theory, the town´s urban layout was determined by two principal axes, the *kardo maximus* and the *decumanus maximus,* at either end of which stood monumental gateways, one of which was the *Arco de Trajano* or Trajan´s Arch.

A second theory, however, defends the concept of the arch being a triumphal construction. The author of this theory was Moreno and its most fervent of exponents, Richmond. In more recent times a

**56.** *An engraving featuring the Temple of Diana.*

Augustan era, and furthermore lay on a perfect axis with regard to the above-mentioned temple, a fact that is of vital importance in any attempt at resolving what is the most problematic aspect of the study of this monument, namely the purpose that it served.

Whereas at first it was thought that the structure of this arch might well be compared to that of the ancient triumphal arches, it was not long before another theory gained the upper hand, namely that which interpreted the arch as nothing less than one of the gateways of the colony, the very one that was to appear on the coins struck in the town and which was to become the emblem of the same. Indeed it was the scholar Mélida who put forward the idea of an *urbs*

new, and in our opinion definitive, interpretation of the arch has been proposed, according to which the function of the latter was to act as an antechamber to a public enclosure of maximum importance, namely the provincial forum, which housed the buildings that served the needs of the subjects of the Province of Lusitania, of which Emerita Augusta was the capital.

The sheer magnificence and the honorific nature of the arch would have sufficed to lend the forum area its own particular character and duly underline the importance of the latter. At the same time, the arch would have acted as a unifying element between different areas of the same town.

## THE TEMPLE OF DIANA

Rising up majestically at the very heart of the town, within the limits of what was once the forum of the colony of Emerita Augusta, are the remains of one of the most remarkable edifices of the town, the so-called *Templo de Diana.*

As one can easily appreciate, a building once occupied a large section of the temple ruins. Erected in the early 16th century, the building came to be known as the *Casa de los Milagros,* or House of the Miracles. Such was the sobriquet that the people of Mérida loved to give to the significant ruins of their town which, simply because they managed to remain upright, never ceased to amaze them.

Remains of the original house, which was subsequently to receive the name of *Palacio de los Corbos,* are to be seen on the principal façade of the building, in the form of a Renaissance-style window featuring certain Gothic additions, above which the family coat of arms is displayed. Moreover, when a part of the old house was pulled down, the courtyard

**57.** *Temple of Diana. Eastern façade together with remains of the Renaissance palace.*

**58.** *Temple of Diana. Present-day condition.*

gallery –whose capitals are decorated with quarters matching those of the coat of arms on the façade– was left open to view. The construction of this stately mansion on the site of the temple prevented any further deterioration of the ancient ruins and consequently the monumental edifice has remained in a good condition right up to the present day.

The façades of the temple were discovered in the course of the excavations carried out from 1972 to 1986, although the eastern façade has yet to be totally unearthed.

The temple is peripteral and hexastyle, that is, it features six columns along its principal façade, and has a more or less north-south orientation. The dimensions of its rectangular ground plan are as follows: the longer sides of the temple measure 31.80 metres (40.75 metres if we are to count the whole length of the border of the construction´s plinth or *podium*), whereas the façades measure 21.90 metres. The entire construction is made of granite from the *Proscrpina* quarries.

The temple colonnade rests on the said plinth, which stands 3.23 metres high from its crown to the base of its socle. The longer sides feature a total of 11 columns. The plinth itself is faced by granite ashlars laid out with alternating headers and stretchers in regular courses, thus forming an excellent example of an *opus quadratum*. The crown of the plinth comprises a cornice featuring ogee moulding or *cyma reversa,* whilst the base ends in a simple, artistic socle adorned with the same type of moulding. Running right round the temple perimeter was an ashlar walkway or border.

The main entrance to the temple, situated at the south façade, opened out onto the present-day *Calle Romero Leal,* and faced the forum square. As far as can be told, it was formed by a small raised surface or landing in the shape of an exedra, from which a staircase led up to the building itself. At the base of the exedra, in the centre, one can still make out traces of an altar.

Inside the temple, the *cella* –the main body where the divinities to whom the temple was dedicated would be worshipped– spanned the area from the fourth to the tenth columns. Today, however, not a single trace of this part of the temple remains.

The columns themselves rest on a series of attic bases which, devoid of plinths, have a stuccoed surface, as do the drums that make up the shafts.

The Corinthian style capitals are each formed by a triple crown of acanthus leaves. In all they stand 0.85 metres high and are entirely decorated in stuccowork.

The elements composing the architrave that supported the temple roof have been well preserved, whilst recently the main pediment was restored, though unfortunately to no great effect. A feature of this pediment was a relieving arch which, in ancient times hidden from view, was situated at its very centre (at the tympanum).

In its day the temple was surrounded by a sacred area or *temenos,* part of which has been successfully reconstructed subsequent to the excavations. The said area, laid out with gardens, was enclosed by a portico and included, both on the western and the eastern sides of the temple, a series of rectangular ponds. Moreover, the latest work carried out at the site has established the existence, on the western side, of the ruins of a cryptoporticus, that is, a subterranean portico.

The structure of the temple at Mérida is comparable to that of other known examples from around the Roman world, and along with the temples at Évora and Barcelona constitutes the only peripteral one (that is, featuring free-standing colonnades) to be found in the Iberian peninsula.

The alleged dedication of the temple to the goddess Diana is purely of an arbitrary nature, even though in past centuries it proved to be extremely popular. The origin of this dedication is to be traced to the work of the local author Moreno de Vargas, who was possibly influenced in his writings by the great fame enjoyed by the temple of the same name in Ephesus. It would seem to be more accurate to think of the temple as a place dedicated to the cult of the emperor, a fact suggested both by its physical situation and by some highly significant finds, amongst which we can cite an image of the Genius of the Senate, which today is on display at the National Museum of Roman Art, and a sedentary sculpture depicting an emperor (probably Claudius), which was discovered late last century and is kept at present at the Archaeological Museum of Seville.

With regard to the possible date at which the temple was constructed, both the architectural features of the latter and the information provided during its excavation lead us to place this event at the final of the Augustean era.

## THE ROMAN HOUSES

At the present point in time we possess only very fragmentary knowledge as to the evolution of the Roman house in Mérida. Whilst on the one hand it is true that during the laying of foundations for the construction of new houses remains pertaining to ancient mansions have come to light, furnishing us with a number of mosaic floorings, some of which are to be seen in the museum, on the other hand we have to admit that our knowledge of such domestic Roman structures is extremely limited.

Nevertheless, the examples that survive to the present day provide us with a satisfactory vision of the development of the Roman house in Mérida from the 1st century to well into the 4th century A.D.

Generally speaking, the items that have been preserved correspond to large mansions that were erected around arcaded courtyards or peristyles designed to supply light to the most important rooms of the edifice. Some of these mansions were to take on truly spectacular dimensions, as is the case with the one situated adjacent to the Amphitheatre. Each and every one of the houses found have surrendered up significant elements of their architectural structure along with examples of the decoration that adorned their walls and floors, namely their frescos and mosaics.

There now follows a description of the most noteworthy illustrations of Roman domestic architecture in Mérida, although it has been necessary for us to overlook many other fine examples, such as those discovered in the *Huerta de Otero* or in *Calle de Suárez Somonte*, which, although no longer present today, were to supply us, respectively, with some interesting mosaics and an exceptional collection of paintings, the latter being on display at the Roman Museum.

### The House of the Amphitheatre

Owing its name to the fact that it is located next to the Roman Amphitheatre, the so-called *Casa del Anfiteatro* is in fact a combination of two houses: on the one hand, the one called *Casa de la Torre del Agua* (or House of the Water Tower), which lies beside a water deposit belonging to the San Lázaro aqueduct, and on the other, the House of the Amphitheatre itself.

Lying adjacent to one of the rows of arches that once made up the said water conduit, at the highest point of the archaeological site and next to the present-day entrance to the *Casa del Anfiteatro* enclosure, are the ruins of the House of the Water Tower.

All that remains of this house are two rooms arranged around an arcaded courtyard or peristyle, which itself has been almost totally destroyed, as have a number of other quarters that would once have formed part of the mansion.

**59.** *Casa del Mitreo*
*(House of the Mithraeum). Cosmogonical mosaic.*

Although it is in a bad state of preservation, we know that the first of the said rooms was of a quadrangular design and was paved with a black and white mosaic dating from the late 1st or early 2nd century A.D., which itself has been almost totally lost. From this room one could enter the second, adjacent room, which lay on a slightly higher level and which today preserves remains of a flooring similar to that of its neighbouring chamber.

The walls of these two rooms retain the remains of painted stuccowork and feature marble slab motifs that describe rectangular compositions with rhomboidal figures.

Very little has survived of what was once the courtyard. All that is to be seen are remains of two of its brick columns faced with stucco and part of the little canal that ran around its entire perimeter. Moreover, several different stages can be observed in the courtyard's construction.

To the south of the courtyard lie other structural elements belonging to the house, amongst which there is another courtyard and additional quarters.

**60.** *House of the Amphitheatre. General view.*

The date of this house was established in the course of the excavations carried out here. It was built in the late 1st century A.D. and was to survive no later than the 3rd century A.D., the time when it would be replaced by the neighbouring House of the Amphitheatre, which we shall now describe. The most striking feature of this structure is its great size. As a result it has been suggested, bearing in mind how near it is to the Amphitheatre itself, that this may have been a building devoted to the education of young people or that it may have been of a semi-official character. However, there is no evidence to support either of these claims.

Judging by the style of the floorings and other details brought to light by the excavations, the construction of this building dates back to the late 3rd century A.D., whilst its demise has to have occurred sometime during the 5th century, owing to the fact that this was when a necropolis was established overlying it. The building lay in a suburban position, that is, outside the walled enclosure, adjacent to the road that led to the Amphitheatre.

Nowadays, entrance is gained to the house by means of a large gate, which bears no relation whatsoever to the original one. The gate opens out into a large, quadrangular room featuring a flooring of brick and lime mortar and walls displaying the remains of their original plastering. From this room, possibly the vestibule, one could pass through into the great peristyle, around which the most important quarters of the house were arranged.

The arcaded courtyard has a garden or *viridarium* at its centre and comprises a series of corridors or passageways supported in their day by granite columns. On three sides of the courtyard, these corridors are paved with mosaics depicting ornamental and geometrical figures, whilst on the other, the flooring is made of brick and lime mortar. The main rooms of the building are seen to open out into these corridors.

Situated on the right-hand side of the building there are two almost symmetrical rooms featuring floors of hydraulic mortar and remains of painted stuccowork on their walls.

Leading off from the western corridor was a higher level of the mansion, on which several rooms were to be found. The two best preserved of these rooms, both of which have brick and lime mortar flooring, open out onto a small corridor. Pictorial decorations were found adorning their walls, which today are in a very bad state of preservation and whose socles are imitations of marble *crustae*.

Returning to the western corridor, we can admire the mosaic that lined its floor and which features a simple cabled frame and a central motif of interlaced swastikas. This corridor led into a series of other rooms with floors of mortar, lime and brick.

Continuing on our tour of the courtyard, we come to the southern wing of the corridor encircling it, which boasts an identical mosaic to that which we have seen in the previous section. Several rooms are seen to run along this side of the corridor, and whilst the larger ones all have excellent features, there is one in particular, in all likelihood a *triclinium* or dining-room, which contains a mosaic of great iconographic interest and a pictorial decoration, very possibly to be attributed to the artist *Quintosus*.

The background of the mosaic comprises red, white and black angles and squares. Its central section features, in one of its two halves or registers, the figures of Venus and Cupid, whilst in the other a wine-making scene is depicted, in which three workers are seen in the process of treading grapes, the fruit of their

**61.** *House of the Mithraeum. Peristyle.*

labour being collected in three bulging recipients. This central scene is surrounded by a series of other images related to the gathering of the grapes, which is performed by small *erotes* pictured climbing up the grapevines on ladders, whilst others transport the harvested bunches back to the wine-press.

This is an excellent quality mosaic, in the fabric of which one can denote contemporary restorations that were performed using tesserae of a lighter hue than the ones originally employed.

From here, a passageway leads us into another part of the house and to a further series of rooms, the excavation of which has not yet been completed and whose floors are paved with mortar. The motif adorning the mosaic in this passageway is that of bichrome squares, each of which contain two red and black triangular segments alternating with white squares that give shape to a series of hour-glasses.

The following wing of the same passageway features another *opus musivum* or mosaic whose pattern is one of red, black and white rhombi.

The passageway finally opens out into another large corridor which likewise has a mosaic flooring. In this case, the pattern of the decorative motif is composed of a succession of white circles surrounded by double axes or astragali joined together around a curvilinear square. The same corridor and mosaic are repeated on the opposite side of the passageway.

Through this corridor we come out into a large antechamber or vestibule belonging to another room of great dimensions. The vestibule is profusely decorated with mosaic, featuring a border with swastika meanders framing five well-defined sections. The outer sections feature fields of crescent-shaped shields, whereas the central ones contain medallions set in square frames. At the heart of the mosaic is a maze of cabling and, lying on either side of the central square are two rosettes of triangles and rhombi. The corners of the squares containing the rosettes are adorned with kraters, whilst those of the maze are graced by tower-shaped structures.

The vestibule is rounded off by another corridor paved with another mosaic whose pattern features a series of squares arranged on end and which is coloured in the following hues: red, black, white-red and black-white.

So great are the proportions of the room we have just referred to –the one lying adjacent to the vestibule– that it ranks as the largest room in the house. The function it fulfilled in ancient times would clearly seem to be that of a reception hall, although bearing in mind the structure of its mosaic,

it could also have acted as the *triclinium* or dining-room.

This mosaic comprises a background that simulates an area paved with large red and black squares and smaller black ones set against a white backing. The centre section features a pattern of squares formed by twisted cables. These squares come together to form eight-pointed stars which in turn mark out a series of octagonal medallions, a number of rhombi and small octagons arising as a result between the different squares. Set within the space outlined by the intertwining squares and framed by circles and undulating designs, are representations of a variety of marine species, amongst which we can identify the sea bream, the hake, the conger eel, the lobster, the sole, the moray and the grouper.

The far end of the house –at least as much of it as has been excavated up to the present day– is taken up by another series of rooms with mosaic flooring which are arranged along a corridor that itself is paved with a mosaic featuring a field of four-petalled flowers and circles containing Maltese crosses.

Completing the group of buildings that go to make up the *Casa del Anfiteatro* is a series of chambers belonging to hot water baths or *thermae* and which were erected here lining the wall of the *San Lázaro* aqueduct. Surviving today is the substructure or *hypocaustum* of a room destined to house a hot water bath (*caldarium*), of which a *piscina*, the oven (*praefurnium*) used to heat the water and other quarters have been preserved.

Adjacent to the hot water baths lie a number of other rooms, amongst which we should highlight a kitchen, preserved along with its fireplace and a variety of serving elements.

### Casa del Mitreo or House of the Mithraeum

This building was found in the early seventies and owes its name to the fact that it lies in the proximity of the ruins of a sanctuary dedicated to Mithras and the eastern gods that was discovered during work on the construction of the nearby *Plaza de Toros* or bullring. Some authors have put forward the idea that this could have been the mansion belonging to the priest who served at the sanctuary, whereas others have gone so far as to claim that it was actually a part of the said place of worship. Whatever function one may wish to assign the building, however, it is clear that it lay in an outlying district of the town.

It would seem that the construction of the building took place in the late 1st century A.D. or at the beginning of the 2nd century A.D. and that it was left to ruin at some time during the 4th or even the 3rd century A.D.

The structure of this remarkable edifice is seen to consist of a number of distinct parts and, as we shall see, the present-day entrance has no connection whatsoever with its original predecessor.

The first of these sections, the nucleus of the building, is arranged around an arcaded courtyard and features a garden *(viridarium)* and a pond which is known to have been flanked by *exedrae* or semicircular benches. Encircling the courtyard is a series of corridors that were originally entirely paved with mosaics, although today the few

turn features a combination of triangles, rhombi and squares of two different sizes. This mosaic, as is the case with those of the adjacent rooms, was made in the 2nd century A.D. The flooring of the room on the left is graced by several bands consisting of frets and meanders and has a central section featuring a square bristling with meanders tracing the shape of swastikas. At the entrance to this room one can still see a carpet composed of four-pointed stars. The main room has its own mosaic which comprises a border of squares set on end and two carpets, the latter featuring a swastika-shaped meander and a border of swastika-shaped meander, respectively. Lying adjacent to these rooms are other highly deteriorated ones.

**62.** *House of the Mithraeum. Cubicula diurna.*

**63.** *House of the Mithraeum. Atrium.*

remains that survive of the latter are limited to the western wing. Giving out onto the said corridors were a number of rooms which we shall now describe to the reader.

The most noteworthy of these rooms are two small ones of similar proportions and the larger room that they flank, the latter possibly having acted as a *triclinium*. The walls of the smaller rooms have socles bearing interesting but highly deteriorated pictorial decorations, one of which features plant and bird motifs. The one situated to the right of the main room was paved with a mosaic flooring that is divided into three sections bordering on a central field which in

In the western corridor, which features the remains of a mosaic whose pattern consisted of squares and rectangles, we come across a large barrel-vaulted cistern, over which another room was erected, a room which when excavated was to provide several valuable pictorial fragments that are now kept at the Museum.

Turning now to the southern corridor, we will be able to make out some other rooms, one of which has an interesting mosaic flooring with a representation of Eros holding a dove.

Carrying on our tour of the *Casa del Mitreo,* we come to an area from which a flight of steps –its walls

**64.** *House of the Amphitheatre. Detail
of the mosaic depicting fish species.*

decorated with paintings imitating streaked marble structures– leads us on to a further two rooms. The purpose that these rooms served in ancient times is not entirely clear, although it has been suggested that they might have been an area *(cubicula diurna)* where one could rest in the summer season.

Located right at the back of the house, next to a Roman road which it would seem might well have been a prolongation of Emerita´s *kardo maximus,* were the bathing facilities. What remains of these today are the oven, the brickwork substructure or *hypocaustum* that once supported one of the rooms of the baths, along with some hot water baths and the room or *caldarium* housing them, the latter paved with a mosaic whose design featured square and right-angled forms.

Another part of the house is seen to revolve around a peristyle containing a pond and lined with columns clad in painted stuccowork.

From the peristyle we can move on to the area of the original entrance to the house, situated in its northern section. Here one can observe a flight of steps crafted in granite ashlars, which allowed one to negotiate the slope between the entrance and the tetrastyle atrium. Arranged around the latter were a number of different rooms. This small atrium or *atriolum,* flanked by granite columns, once boasted a little pond or *impluvium* lined with moulded marble.

To the east of the atrium one can make out granite doorjambs belonging to a series of outbuildings that have yet to be properly excavated.

On the opposite side, occupying a well-centred position with regard to the atrium, is a room where the so-called *Mosaico Cósmico* or Cosmic Mosaic was discovered, in all likelihood one of the most important mosaics of the Roman world. The interior of this room clearly reveals the characteristic features of its structure, namely the rubblework socle and the adobe elevation, the corners of which are reinforced with ashlars. The walls were decorated with paintings that have partially been preserved.

The mosaic itself constitutes a complete allegorical representation of the cosmos. Presiding the composition is the figure of Time and his sons, Heaven and Chaos, next to which appear the Titans Pole and Thunder, sons of Heaven and Earth. Placed around these are the figures of the Sun, the Moon, the Winds and the Clouds. At the centre of the mosaic there is an image of *Aion,* Eternity, together with those of Nature, the Seasons, the Mountain and the Snow.

An outstanding feature of the mosaic, likewise situated at the centre of the composition, is the beautiful figure of Aurora *(Oriens),* who is depicted commanding her chariot, ready to traverse the celestial vault.

In its lower section, the colouring of which features very effective shades of green and blue, the watery element appears personified in the form of the rivers (the Nile and the Euphrates), a Port, the Lighthouse, the Sea and Navigation.

Every aspect of the composition is perfect, from the quality of its design to the nuances of the human body and the variety of hues used for the different areas of the mosaic. Furthermore, the various elements of nature depicted are identified by their Latin names. Only materials of the highest quality were employed in the creation of the mosaic, and the artists responsible were even to resort to tesserae of transparent glass containing a thin sheet of gold in order to enhance certain ornamental accessories worn by the figures, such as torques, bracelets, or the crown adorning the beautiful figure of *Oriens.*

The whole mosaic is an allegory, for this is the simplest way of explaining the phenomena of nature.

Outside the room containing the Mosaic of the Cosmos, on its external walls, remains of pictorial decoration are to be found.

A small flight of granite steps takes us on to the adjoining area, on the right-hand side of which we can witness another of the remarkable legacies of the *Casa del Mitreo,* namely the "Room of the Paintings", so called due to its outstanding pictorial decoration. Its socle features plant and bird motifs, whereas the central section of the wall displays several fields separated by candelabra.

## THE BRIDGE
## OVER THE RIVER GUADIANA

The undeniable rôle played by the bridge over the river Guadiana in determining both the eventual location of the Roman town of *Emerita Augusta* and the urban layout of the same would seem to imply that this is the oldest monument to be found in Mérida and one of the most significant elements of the town´s archaeological heritage.

The bridge was built at the point of the river that offered the most favourable topographical conditions for the enterprise, at a place where the river flow was at its weakest and was broken by an island. Work on its construction was completed at the first attempt and was not spread over three phases as was previously believed. Today the bridge is 792 metres long.

The structure of the bridge consisted of two arched sections joined by a solid section protected by an enormous cutwater.

The first section of the bridge´s fabric spanned the space between the town walls and the part that today constitutes the first path leading down from the bridge. This section is the best preserved of all, due to the fact that it is situated in the smallest arm of the river and

**65.** *Roman bridge over the river Guadiana.*

therefore has been less exposed to the violent force of its currents. In order to span the said space, ten arches were erected over a total of nine foundational piers equipped with rounded cutwaters, eight of which remain in good condition today. Furthermore, the piers are pierced by a series of little relief arches or spillways, the purpose of which is to enable the current to pass the bridge at times of high water.

The second section stretched from the present-day abutment-pier, built in the 19th century, to the end of the bridge and today presents a total of fifty arches.

The piers and arches making up the bridge in this section, which runs as far as the second of the paths leading down from the bridge, display identical characteristics to those of the first section explained above. As from this path onwards, however, the piers are seen to have neither spillways nor cutwaters, a fact which is easily explained if one bears in mind that only in times of severe flooding would the water reach this part of the bridge.

The bridge construction features a core of Roman concrete faced with granite extracted from nearby quarries. The ashlars lining the triangular faces of the piers are arranged in extremely regular courses interspersed by the voussoirs of the main arches and those of the relieving arches or spillways. A notable feature of the bridge is the rustication of these ashlars, an effect which breaks up the otherwise monotonous pier faces and gives rise to some quite outstanding combinations of light and shade.

Turning our attention back to the structure of the piers, the latter are seen to have taken on a rectangular shape and were conferred a substantial width owing both to the span of the arches they supported and to the precarious nature of certain areas of the bridge foundations. As has already been mentioned, the cutwaters generally have a rounded shape, although in the modern sections of the bridge they adopt either a pyramidal structure –in the parts affected by the reforms undertaken in the 17th century– or a conical shape crowned by a pointed cap –in the section dating from the 19th century.

The arches spring from a series of slightly projecting imposts that in turn constitute the crowning course of the piers. The voussoirs that go to make up the arches are uniform in shape, whilst the keystones are well-defined. The extrados of each of the arches stands out clearly, as does the intrados, although neither projects beyond the surface of the pier face.

Nothing more than a few fragments remain of the original cornice of the bridge, the element which crowned the ashlar courses and marked the beginning of the parapet.

However, the most extraordinary feature of the bridge´s architecture was the cutwater shielding the mole that joined the two sections of arches. Having been destroyed in the course of the centuries, today the ruins of this cutwater are to be seen scattered amongst the gravel on the island that lies further upstream. The description of the cutwater provided by the local historian Moreno de Vargas paints us a clear picture as to its structure: "the wall that delimited it extended upstream and its construction featured a prow similar to that of a galley placed at its head, so that at times of both ordinary and great floods all the strength and the fury of the swift river current would be spent here, and the waters reaching the arches that lay behind it on either side would be calmer... In this way both the safety of the bridge and the uniformity of its breadth and surface were assured".

Being a construction of great significance and fulfilling as it did such an eminently utilitarian purpose, the Roman bridge at Mérida was to be damaged on numerous occasions as a result of both flooding and wars. Repairs to the bridge would normally be carried out immediately after any such event, depending on the circumstances prevailing at the time. By virtue of the records held at the Municipal Historical Archive, several of the restoration projects undertaken can be documented.

Amongst the most important of these restoration programmes are those dating from Visigothic times –an inscription tells us of the restoration carried out in the year 483 during the reign of Euric–, from the period of Arab rule in Spain and from the 16th, 17th and 19th centuries. The most far-reaching of the reconstructions were those of the 17th century –in which, subsequent to the destruction of the cutwater, the two sides of the bridge were joined by means of a five new arches– and the 19th century, when a large section of the present-day fabric of the bridge was built.


THE BRIDGE
OVER THE RIVER ALBARREGAS

The bridge over the river Albarregas –the source of which is to be found in the vicinity of the Cornalvo reservoir– is a rather modest structure when compared with the one spanning the Guadiana and has never been truly considered as constituting one of the elements of the monumental architecture of the town. Very few details are known regarding either its history or the restoration work that has been carried out on its fabric.

This bridge marked the beginning of the *Vía de la Plata* or Silver Route and its orientation to some extent influenced the final course drawn by Emerita's *kardo maximus*.

Subsequent to the restoration that it has undergone in modern times, the bridge now has a length of 145 metres, whilst the width of the road crossing it is approximately 8 metres.

The first section of the bridge features a modern parapet faced with ashlars laid out horizontally, along with a recently added cornice and petril. The presence of two spillways or floodwater outlets –which underwent reconstruction sometime during the last century– testify to the violent nature of the river flow at times of flooding. Further along, completing the

The piers of this bridge, featuring as they do well-structured facings comprising as a rule eleven courses of ashlar, are equipped with neither cutwaters nor spillways due to the fact that the latter are simply not necessary here.

The triangular sections of the bridge face situated between each pair of arches has been largely preserved and feature rusticated ashlars in perfect harmony with the arch voussoirs.

The bridge, which can be considered as dating from the last quarter of the 1st century B.C., reaches its end at another, largely modern parapet featuring rubblework facings.

**66.** *The ground plan and the elevation of the bridge over the river Albarregas.*

structure of the bridge, is a series of four arches by means of which the waters of the Albarregas are crossed.

All four arches are identical as regards their structural characteristics and are in a good state of repair. They are all semicircular in form, their spans ranging in size from 5.2 metres (the first arch) to 3.8 (the fourth one). Just like the arches of the Guadiana Bridge, they are seen to spring from a series of bases, although in this case the latter are not quite so pronounced. The arches are composed of a variable number of voussoirs, the keystones being well-defined and the intrados barely noticeable. Some of the voussoirs have a rusticated finish.

## THE "ALCANTARILLA ROMANA" OR LITTLE ROMAN BRIDGE

A third bridge was built by the Romans along the road that led to *Olisipo* (Lisbon), at a point about 500 metres from the district called *Las Abadías* in the proximity of the Albarregas bridge, or to be more precise, between kilometres 454 and 455 of the railway line to Badajoz.

This single-spanned bridge is 7 metres long and has a width of 4.35 metres, or 6 metres if we include the parapets on either side. It is easy to see that the bridge has been restored on many occasions, as a result of which its original character has been

**67.** *The bridge called Alcantarilla Romana or Little Roman Bridge.*

**68.** *Fountain and arch curvature at the House of the Amphitheatre.*

impaired somewhat. Nevertheless, at the part of the bridge that faces upstream one can clearly distinguish the peculiar features characterizing its construction, which are similar to those described above in relation to the other two bridges of Emerita. Whilst the core of its structure is made of concrete, the arch itself comprises a series of rusticated granite voussoirs and springs from a modest ashlar base.

The parapet dates from modern times, as do certain other parts of the bridge´s fabric that are made of brick. One can easily appreciate the characteristics of the Roman road –which has since been reconstructed–, both on the bridge itself and in the surrounding area.

## AQUEDUCTS AND RESERVOIRS

As soon as the town of *Emerita Augusta* had been founded, the Romans´ utilitarian spirit was to come to the fore in the shape of plans for the construction of no less than three water conduits. Large sections of the ruins of these aqueducts have survived to the present day and in themselves bear witness to the great effort that was made to provide sufficient water supplies to residential areas of the newly-established colony. Such constructions as these are a reflection of the atmosphere of magnificence and great faith in the future that characterized the master touches of Augustan urban development.

### The Cornalvo Aqueduct

The first such water conduit to be built, whose name in Roman times was *Aqua Augusta* –as we are attaining a maximum height of 18 metres. Conferred a sloping design in order to better resist the thrust of the waters, the structural features of this dam are similar to those of other constructions –both of this type and of a defensive nature– dating from the end of the Republic and the dawning of the Empire. Its fabric is made up of a massive earth filling that was used to reinforce the actual dam structure, which itself features a concrete core faced with small, roughly hewn masonry.

**69.** *Cornalvo Reservoir.*

informed by an inscription kept in the National Museum of Roman Art–, is referred to today as the *Cornalvo* Aqueduct. It is thus called owing to the fact that it originates at a reservoir of that very name situated about 15 kilometres to the north-east of the town.

Still surviving at the said reservoir, in an excellent condition subsequent to the alterations carried out a few years ago, is the dam that was constructed in order to close off the reservoir basin, the total perimeter of the latter measuring some 10 kilometres. The dam wall, which itself stretches out over 220 metres, was erected between two gently rising hills,

Standing at the centre of the dam and largely submerged in the water is a square-shaped tower measuring 9.5 metres across and 20 metres high, in which the gates regulating the water flow along the conduit are housed. The tower is faced in rusticated granite ashlars laid out in courses featuring alternating headers and stretchers; its structure is in fact very similar to that observed in the earliest monuments to be raised in Emerita, namely the Roman Bridge and Amphitheatre. In former times the walkway leading from the dam to the tower was supported by an arch comprising voussoirs crafted from this very same material. Nowadays, however, although the

**70.** *San Lázaro Aqueduct.*

components of the ancient arch have been preserved, the latter has been replaced by an ugly metal structure.

Leaving the reservoir from the bottom of the tower, the water would run along a sturdily-built granite ashlar channel measuring 1.7 metres high and 0.7 metres wide.

At a point 300 metres along its course, this general conduit was joined by another one which, originating in *El Borbollón,* an area situated 3 kilometres to the north, supplied a considerable amount of water. Throughout the *Campomanes* country estate, large sections of this second channel still survive, its structure featuring rubblework and semicircular arches.

Thus the Cornalvo aqueduct made its way across the lands surrounding Emerita, basically following the course of the river Albarregas, until it finally came to the town. A variety of topographical obstacles, such as valley depressions or watercourses, were overcome in some cases by the construction of arcades and other structural solutions, and in others by altering the course of the channel, as a result of which certain sections of the aqueduct trace a truly winding outline. Of particular importance are the remains that, as one approaches Mérida, are to be found adjacent to the Psychiatric Hospital, and which are known by the eloquent name of *Caño Quebrado* or Broken Pipe.

Having covered a distance of nearly 25 kilometres, the water conduit finally arrived at the eastern limits of the town of Mérida. It then passed through part of the necropolis called *Los Bodegones,* and entered the walled enclosure at the ancient Municipal Water Deposit. Large sections of the aqueduct featuring a vaulted roof structure have recently been discovered in this area, leading towards the Roman Theatre, which it thus supplied with water. In spite of this, the main channel continued its course on the other side of the town walls and, passing through the necropolis called *Los Columbarios,* ended up at the great terminal deposit or *castellum aquae,* which was seemingly located in the vicinity of the bullring.

### The San Lázaro Aqueduct

The source of the second aqueduct to be built in Emerita, which nowadays is known under the name of *Rabo de Buey-San Lázaro,* was situated some 5 kilometres to the north of the town. Here, on the country estates of *Casa Herrera, Las Tomas* and *Valhondo,* a number of subterranean springs and water currents were found which, once they had been properly channelled, were to furnish the great bulk of the water transported by this particular conduit. Moreover, just as we have seen in the case of the Cornalvo aqueduct, the San Lázaro structure was further supplied by other abundant sources, the channels of which are largely still preserved today.

The course followed by the aqueduct covered a distance of 4 kilometres and today its well-preserved remains constitute a truly spectacular sight. The row of arches that goes to make up the main section of its fabric is seen to reach a great height; built in stone rubblework, it features semicircular arches and masonry courses of the same material. Spread out at regular intervals along the course of the channel, there was a series of square-shaped ports or outlets intended for cleaning purposes. These outlets were sealed by means of granite ashlars and were accompanied by entrances to the channel that were reached by means of regularly spaced flights of steps. The water channel itself, or *specus,* was 0.6 metres wide and was lined with a layer of hydraulic mortar.

Emerging on the country estate called *La Godina,* the aqueduct came to an end at the deposit known as *Rabo de Buey,* situated at the highest point of the present-day district of *La Paz,* where presumably there would have been a sedimentation tank or *piscina limaria* for the purification of the water. Sadly, the final part of this section of the aqueduct has been largely destroyed and one can observe, next to the modern conduit, the remains of the ancient channel.

The whole course of this aqueduct, right from its very source, was repaired at the end of the last century, thanks to the efforts of the then mayor of Mérida and great publicist, Pedro María Plano. The aim behind the project was that water should reach Mérida just as it had done in Roman times, an aim that was fulfilled up until only quite recently.

The great obstacle that faced this aqueduct right from the outset, namely the Albarregas river valley, a depression of quite considerable width, was overcome by means of the construction of a series of high arches joining the pillars that supported the channel. In its day, this part of the aqueduct was a truly magnificent structure measuring over a kilometre in length, although all that remains of it today are three pillars and a series of granite ashlar arches, elements that afford the same characteristics as those of the *Los Milagros* Aqueduct, which we will describe presently. It was at this point that the Roman road uniting Emerita with *Toletum* (Toledo) and *Corduba* (Córdoba) passed under the aqueduct.

Within the area of the so-called House of the Amphitheatre, an interesting sedimentation and distribution tower was discovered. Rectangular in design, this tower was built using a mixture of different masonry forms, such as ashlar, rubblework and brick, the latter material also being employed in the

**71.** *Bridge Over the River Albarregas
and Los Milagros Aqueduct,
depicted in an engraving by Laborde.*

**72.** *Los Milagros Bridge and Aqueduct.*

construction of its vaulted roof. Inside, its walls were decorated with paintings. Standing 4.8 metres at its highest point, the tower has a width of 2.3 metres.

The exact location of the terminal deposit or *castellum* of the aqueduct is not known, although it is believed that it cannot have been far from the tower. Be that as it may, when excavations were carried out on the site known as *Las Torres,* the one on which the National Museum of Roman Art was to be built, a sizeable section of the aqueduct was uncovered. Rising up to a considerable height and featuring an outlet or *spiramen,* the said section once led on to the centre of the town, which was the principal area it was designed to provide with water. However, it also supplied the buildings dedicated to public spectacles, the Amphitheatre and the Theatre, although these were also fed by the Cornalvo aqueduct.

In the 16th century, to be precise in the year 1504, by which time the conduit already lay in ruins, the

**73.** Detail of
Los Milagros
Aqueduct.

town authorities decided to construct another water channel, which was to be referred to as the Renaissance Aqueduct or that of San Lázaro, in order to ensure that Mérida would not suffer any water shortage. The course of this aqueduct is parallel to that of the Roman construction, and it is to be seen running alongside the surviving pillars of the latter in the Albarregas valley. Its structure, however, was to turn out to be far from practical, since after a time the clay pipes along which the water was carried became blocked due to the accumulation of deposits, and as a result the aqueduct fell into disuse.

### The Proserpina or "Los Milagros" Aqueduct

Of all the Roman aqueducts that once graced the town of Emerita, this is the one that features the best-preserved remains. Its source was to be found in the reservoir called *Albuera de Carija,* which in the 18th century, subsequent to the discovery of a memorial stone dedicated to the Lusitanian goddess Proserpine, was to change its name in favour of the latter. The reservoir is situated 5 kilometres to the north of the town and can be reached by means of a narrow but well-paved road that leads off from a junction on the present-day road from Mérida to Montijo. Both rainwater and the waters provided by nearby streams such as that called *Las Pardillas* accumulated in the reservoir basin, the perimeter of which measured approximately 5 kilometres. In order to make the best use of the said water, a wide range of channels were built which can still be seen today.

This reservoir was engineered using a series of highly interesting construction techniques. As was the case with the above-mentioned Cornalvo Reservoir, it

**74.** *Proserpina Reservoir.*

features a massive earthen fill and a sloping dam comprising a concrete core and a facing of small, roughly hewn ashlars.

The dam itself is about 500 metres long and has an elevation of some 7 metres with regard to the average water level of the reservoir. The integrity of the dam was assured by virtue of both the basic structure of the wall and the presence of a number of buttresses which, rectangular in section, rose to a height greater than that of the wall itself. The present-day appearance of the dam is due largely to the reconstruction work undertaken on it in the 17th century. To be seen embedded in the dam wall are two square-shaped turrets that were also rebuilt at that time and which, equipped with stairs, lead down to the foot of the dam where the sluice gates controlling the flow of water into the channel are located. Recently, subsequent to the draining of the basin, studies have been carried out on the dyke, leading to the discovery of a previously unknown lower section that features a series of rounded Augustan cutwaters.

From this point, the course followed by the conduit on its way to the town measured about 9 kilometres and wherever possible took advantage of favourable contours in order to guarantee a smooth water flow.

On the country estates called *El Cuarto de la Charca, Carija* and *La Calera,* significant remains of the aqueduct are still to be found. At the first of these locations, recent excavations have revealed that the channel once passed over a sizeable mass of granitic rock, a feat which would have implied a great amount of work to achieve.

In order to overcome the obstacle presented by valley bottoms, a number of rows of tall arches were erected. Although these structures have disappeared in the course of time, their bases have been preserved, and can be seen at the above-mentioned estates. Unfortunately, the water channel itself, which in its day was covered by a small brick or stone vault –the choice of material varying from one area to another–, does not remain intact and in more recent times has incomprehensibly been further destroyed as a result of the construction of a section of the dual-carriageway leading from Madrid to Badajoz.

Near the town cemetery, in the *Santa Eulalia* district, the ruins still survive of a sedimentation tank or *piscina limaria* featuring a sluice gate chamber and

**75.** *The Terminal Water Deposit or Castellum Aquae of the Los Milagros Aqueduct.*

an upper outlet in the form of a spillway. From this point on, the aqueduct is seen to gain height in order to once again negotiate the obstacle provided by the Albarregas valley.

This arched section of the aqueduct, running from the said sedimentation tank to the terminal located on *El Cerro del Calvario* (Calvary Hill), is 827 metres long and rises to a maximum height of 25 metres.

Its structure demonstrates the sheer perfection and mastery that Roman engineers were to achieve in the solutions they found for this kind of architectural construction. It basically consists of a series of pillars, each of which features a sturdy concrete core and is clad in ashlar and brick, the latter materials being arranged in alternating layers of 5 courses each. The pillars themselves measure 3 metres across and occasionally boast a 2 metre-wide and 2.5 metre-deep sloping buttress.

Generally speaking, the pillars are linked by means of a series of arches fashioned in brick, although the ones joining the pillars that flank the River Albarregas are made of ashlar.

The water channel, or *specus,* was situated along the top of the said arches.

The Proserpina aqueduct –which in centuries past was the cause of general amazement amongst the inhabitants of Mérida, who believed the fact that the pillars remained upright to be a miracle, hence the other name by which it is known, *Los Milagros*– has managed to survive right up to the present day in what can be described as an excellent condition. A total of 73 pillars remain, in varying stages of deterioration, and, owing to the sheer monumentality of its structure, the *Los Milagros* Aqueduct ranks as the second most important edifice of the historical ensemble of Mérida, surpassed only by the Roman Theatre itself.

Some years ago work was carried out on the aqueduct in order to strengthen and restore several of its arches and the cornice crowning its pillars.

The aqueduct structure came to an end at one of the town´s highest points, namely *El Cerro del Calvario* (Calvary Hill), where in the early nineteen-seventies the ruins of its terminal deposit were found. This impressive water deposit can be easily seen today, lying as it does adjacent to the little hermitage belonging to the confraternity of the Calvary, in the street that bears the same name *(Calle Calvario).*

The deposit as such is in a bad state of repair, but nevertheless one can make out the basic components of its structure. Its interior features a series of marble-lined sedimentation steps, whilst the general features of its construction are seen to be similar to those already mentioned with regard to the aqueduct´s raised arches, the alternating layers of brick and rough hewn ashlar courses being repeated here.

One of the most controversial aspects surrounding the aqueducts of Emerita Augusta is the determination of the respective dates at which they were built. In spite of the fact that as yet no comprehensive study has been carried out covering the entire layout of the aqueduct system, an enterprise that would imply the undertaking of further relevant excavations, it is perhaps possible to establish the correct date of construction of these great masterpieces of engineering simply by taking into account the indications given by the characteristics of their individual structures. Opinions, however, still remain divided.

Thus, for some authors, the aqueducts clearly belong to the Augustan period, whereas others prefer

**76.** *Remains of the water channel.*

to place them in the 2nd century and still others –though not quite so many– have attributed them to the 4th century A.D. Generally speaking, and even though a succession of structural alterations are to be seen in its fabric, the impression given by this magnificent ensemble is that its construction was indeed carried out during the reign of Augustus.

The Cornalvo Aqueduct, bearing in mind the features of the construction of its dam and the fact that we have in our possession an inscription recording its former name, *Aqua Augusta,* would seem to be easily attributable to the said period.

The same is true of the Rabo de Buey-San Lázaro Aqueduct, where excavations have brought to light a number of items that unmistakeably belong to the Augustan era.

Of a more problematic nature, on the other hand, is the Proserpina-Milagros Aqueduct. Even though this conduit is the one that has been studied in greater detail due to the abundance of its remains, no reliable data –of the type that could be obtained by means of excavations– has as yet been found. Nevertheless, the most recent studies on this particular aqueduct confirm it as belonging to the same period of time.

**77.** *Exterior view of the Alange spa.*

## THE ROMAN BATHS AT ALANGE

At the nearby village of Alange, 18 kilometres from Mérida, lie the eloquent remains of an extensive Roman baths complex, which owing to its historical importance has been declared a National Monument.

The spa, in ancient times referred to as *Aquae,* was in all likelihood abandoned during the Middle Ages, but subsequently returned to its original use as from the 18th century, when new quarters were built alongside the Roman remains, conferring it with the appearance it affords today.

The spring supplying the spa, whose highly radioactive waters emerge at a temperature of 28° C and whose flow rate has been measured at 216 litres per minute, is of exceptional quality. The specific properties of these waters are especially recommended for sufferers of nervous diseases, who come here in great numbers during the bathing season.

**78 and 79.** *The Central Chamber.*
*An old engraving and its*
*present-day appearance.*

73

The group of buildings that go to make up the spa occupy a large area of land, and as a result it is possible to take a long, pleasant walk around the modern quarters and the Roman structure. Seen from the outside, the Roman section is irregular in shape and offers the visitor no clue as to the sheer magnificence that awaits him in its interior.

The Roman hot water baths are housed in a rectangular building, the longer sides of which measure 33 metres, and the shorter ones 16 metres. The building faces from east to west and comprises two rotundas or twin chambers.

A steeply rising staircase, erected in modern times against one of the shorter sides of the building, leads the visitor to the baths up to a barrel-vaulted corridor in which the entrances to the bathing chambers themselves are to be found.

Still in use today, these chambers feature the same structural characteristics and are equal in size, measuring 10.9 metres in diameter and standing 13.86 metres high. At the centre of each chamber there is a circular bathing pool or *piscina,* complete with steps leading down into the water. Both chambers are covered by a vault in the shape of a hemispherical dome, the centre of which has been perforated by an *oculus* or circular opening. In their day, the vaults were decorated by means of paintings, some traces of which were still to be noticed at the end of the 18th century.

**80.** *Present-day entrance to the baths.*

**81.** *Votive altar or ara dedicated to the goddess Juno at the baths.*

Arranged symmetrically around the walls of each bathing room are four exedras, the forms of which are reminiscent of apses or niches. The dimensions of some of these recesses appear to have been altered as a result of the construction of screens, which were introduced in order to use this space as changing areas for the bathers. The original purpose of the exedras was simply an architectural one, constituting as they do the load-bearing supports of the vaults.

In the spa courtyard, set in the face of the eastern wall, next to the area of modern individual baths, there is a votive ara or altar that was dedicated to the goddess *Iuno Regina* by Licinius Serenianus, senator and in all likelihood the governor of Cappadocia in the year 235, and his wife, Varinia Etaccina, for the sake of the health of their daughter Varinia Serena.

Lying adjacent to the spa is the hermitage of *El Cristo de los Baños,* a highly revered institution both in the village and amongst the bathers, which was erected over what was possibly a site of Roman worship and which had served the same function in Visigothic times. The outstanding feature of the hermitage church is the well-crafted image of its patron, the Most Holy Christ of the Baths.

Judging by the constructional features of its fabric, the spa could well have been built in the 1st century A.D., during the Flavian era.

# CHRISTIAN MÉRIDA

## THE VISIGOTHIC COLLECTION

The archaeological finds dating from the Visigothic era that once formed part of the collections kept at the old Roman Museum in Mérida are now housed at the church of the convent of *Santa Clara,* which, situated in the proximity of the *Plaza de España,* was once home to the said museum. They constitute a collection of exceptional value, which in due course will surely be put on show in the modern exhibition facilities they truly deserve, instead of at the current, severely limited premises.

As from the late 5th century, the former *Emerita* was to experience a period of uncommon splendour. Ecclesiastical power, which by then had already become firmly established in Mérida, would prove to be the driving force behind all political, economic and social activity in the town, as is clearly illustrated in an anonymous contemporary work of art entitled *Lives of the Fathers of the Church in Mérida.* From an analysis of the said work it can be deduced that at that time there existed a wealthy, thriving society whose fortune was founded on the brisk trade it developed with the various towns of the former Roman Empire.

So great was the power of the Church in Mérida –a power wielded by its three great personalities, Paulo, Fidel and Massona– that in the times of King Leovigild the civil authorities had to abandon their attempt at making Mérida the administrative capital of the kingdom and resign themselves to staying in Toledo.

It should come as no surprise that such an atmosphere was to stimulate an uncommonly intense artistic activity in the town, which in turn would give rise to the creation of a new art style, namely the Hispanic art of the Visigothic era.

A number of essential elements were seen to contribute to the evolution of Visigothic plastic art in Mérida, namely the Hispano-Roman tradition, the perfectly crafted art forms from the Constantinople area, along with others that, having originated in the Byzantine world, had been reinterpreted in a variety of ancient Italian towns, above all in Ravenna. Other influences at work were those emanating from the north of Africa, as well as the strictly oriental artistic currents that arrived in Spain via the trade routes with Byzantium.

Thus it is clear for all to see that the inhabitants of Mérida in Visigothic times led a very prosperous existence, a fact which is confirmed by the archaeological remains that have been discovered.

**82.** *Visigothic collection. General view.*

This collection of Visigothic items –which unfortunately we cannot call the Visigothic Museum, since this has yet to be created– is the most important of its kind existing on the Iberian Peninsula. The collection began to take shape as from the 16th century and was subsequently to be enriched as a result of the numerous finds made over the past centuries and above all those items unearthed in the course of the systematic excavations carried out in the area of the Moslem fortress or *Alcazaba,* in San Pedro de Mérida and at the basilica situated on the country capitals, all of which are to be attributed to several different centuries, principally the 6th and the 7th.

Worthy of special mention are the stone screens which, dating from the same period, bear witness to the quality of the sculptors at work in Mérida, who had the necessary skills to create a wide range of both plant motifs and highly symbolic animal forms.

A number of objects have also been preserved pertaining to the early liturgy of Mérida, such as altar supports, featuring *loculi* or niches to hold relics, altar slabs like the one from the *Casa Herrera* country estate

**83.** *Inscription alluding to the dedication of a church to the Blessed Virgin Mary.*

estate of *Casa Herrera.* Amongst the items on display, arranged as they are in accordance with the space and the structure of the nave in which they are kept, some are of particular importance.

Of particular interest in the collection is a series of architectural elements from a variety of civil and religious buildings of which we hold very little information, since many of these objects had apparently been re-used in constructions dating from modern times. Examples of these elements are pilasters featuring extremely beautiful plant-motif decoration, pilasters of smaller proportions and cyma recta

that bears an inscription, as well as prismatic altars in which relics were kept.

Amongst the inscriptions in the collection there is a large amount of tombstones on which, using expressions in use at that time, the names of the deceased are recorded along with the date of their demise.

In addition, there are other inscriptions referring to buildings and churches, such as the one alluding to the consecration of the church dedicated to the Virgin Mary and All Virgins, in which a fair number of relics were kept, amongst them those of St James and of the Lord´s Cross itself.

**84, 85 and 86.** *Screens and a niche from the Visigothic collection.*

Completing this impressive ensemble of remains testifying to the Visigothic era is a number of other significant items, such as a niche in the form of an arch with a vaulted scallop decorated with Christ's monograph, from which the letters alpha and omega are seen to hang, and a 6th century baptismal font.

Kept in a series of glass showcases is an array of ceramic utensils of different kinds (small vases, clay lamps decorated with Christian motifs), along with various metal objects, stone plates with reliefs, and decorated bricks.

**87.** *The Basilica at Casa Herrera country estate.*

## THE PALAEOCHRISTIAN BASILICA AT CASA HERRERA

This building, situated some 7 kilometres to the north of Mérida on a small hill whose sides slope gently away to the south and the west (38º 55´ N, 2º 37´ W), was discovered and partially excavated in 1943 by J. de C. Serra Rafols. At a later date, T. Ulbert undertook the task of cleaning the remains and furnishing them with documentary evidence, and in the years 1971 and 1972, accompanied by L. Caballero Zoreda, carried out excavation campaigns, one in each year, as a result of which the monument would take on the appearance it affords today.

The fabric of the basilica, whose plan is almost square in shape, being slightly narrower to the east, is composed of a nave and three aisles divided by six columns. The outermost of these columns stand very close to the triumphal arch of the apses, which in turn are slightly stilted and are seen to project out at either end of the east-west axis.

The base of this construction is formed by a series of rubblework walls that contain a certain amount of brick and which in turn lie on foundations consisting of a double-sided even layer of mortar filled with another less stable material. In some sections of the said foundations and at the corners of the building, granite ashlars are to be seen. The basilica has a total length of 34 metres and reaches a maximum width, on its eastern side, of 22 metres.

The building itself can be divided into two sections: the basilica itself featuring a nave and two aisles, and the other quarters surrounding these.

The two-aisled nave features an eastern apse whose inner length is 5.5 metres and which is 5 metres wide. The western apse, on the other hand, measures only 4.75 by 4.65 metres. In its day the nave, which is seen to become narrower as it runs from east to west (5.35 m - 4.65 m), was separated from its aisles by a series of 12 white marble columns which, each crafted from a single piece of stone, were placed on Corinthian bases featuring three mouldings, some of which were found *in situ*. Remaining intact in the northern aisle is the 2.2-metre wide entrance to the basilica, flanked by ashlars forming its walls and having a marble threshold that has been preserved in its original position.

The adjacent quarters comprise seven little cubicles measuring approximately 4 by 4 metres. The shape of these rooms was to be greatly modified in the course of the successive alterations that the building underwent throughout its history, and the purpose that either of them may have once served remains to be clearly established, although without doubt it would seem that they were connected in some way with the liturgical function of the basilica. Worthy of special mention amongst these quarters is the one located in the north-eastern section of the church, which appears to have acted as a baptistery and whose construction reveals two distinct stages, a first one in which a deep rectangular font was used, and a second stage marked by the addition of two small stoups placed adjacent to each other.

In its original form the entire flooring of the basilica was made of ceramic slabs, some sections of which were subsequently replaced by *opus signium* mosaic; the said paving was to be totally destroyed as a result of the burials that took place inside the basilica as from the 6th century. All in all and in light of the data revealed by the excavation campaigns, it can be claimed that the basilica was built, in accordance with African models (a feature of which are the mutually opposing apses), in around the year 500 A.D. Two clearly distinguishable phases are to be identified in its construction, namely a first stage featuring the erection of the nave and two aisles, including the mutually opposing apses and the columns separating the nave from the aisles, and a second phase, possibly dating from the second half of the 6th century, in which the baptistery and the adjoining quarters were built.

**88.** *The walls of the Alcazaba.*

# MOSLEM MÉRIDA

### THE ALCAZABA OR FORTRESS

Lying very near the Plaza de España to the south of the old town centre is the Moslem monument *par excellence* of the town of Mérida, namely its *Alcazaba,* one side of which is flanked by the river Guadiana, which thus provides the structure with a natural form of defence.

The *Alcazaba* is a fortress whose plan takes the shape of a quadrilateral, the sides of which measure between 132 and 137 metres. Its 580-metre long perimeter is encircled by walls whose average thickness is 2.7 metres. The basic elements used in its construction were granite ashlars –most of which were taken from the ancient Roman buildings– laid out in horizontal courses and bedded in an abundant mixture of ashlar waste, mortar and earth.

A total of 25 quadrangular towers were spaced out at regular intervals around the *alcazaba*, the best preserved sections of which feature towers that rise to a height of 15 metres. In former times, access to the interior of the fortress was gained by means of at least three gateways, the present-day entrance being merely the result of the deliberate mutilation of one of the walls that was performed earlier this century.

Adjoining the *alcazaba* was a smaller enclosure designed to defend the nearby bridge. Measuring 20 by 23 metres, it featured a total of four gates. Recent excavations carried out beneath this enclosure have unearthed traces both of the original Roman gateway that once protected the entrance to the town from this point, and of a road with a lane in either direction, just like the one leading through the gate that appears engraved on the local coins dating from the Augustan and Tiberian eras.

A marble slab positioned over the gateway that leads into the grounds of the *alcazaba* from the bridge provides us with certain details concerning the construction of the fortress.

Martín Almagro has transcribed the inscription as follows:

"In the name of Allah, the Clement and the Merciful. May the blessing of Allah and protection come to all those who are in obedience of Allah".

"This fortress was commissioned and fortified as a place of refuge for those who obey Him by the emir Abd al-Rahman II, son of Al-Hakam –may Allah glorify him–, under the direction of his architect Abd Allah, son of Kulaid, son of Tálaba and of Gaifar, son of Mukassir, his freedman and director of the construction, in Rabi II of the (Islamic) year 220 (835 of the Christian era)".

Any visit to the *alcazaba* starts at the gateway that was artificially opened up in the wall furthest away from the river. Taking a path that leads gently down towards the river, we pass on our right the remains of a sumptuous Roman mansion which, dating from the Lower Empire, lies framed by two ancient urban roads.

Still surviving in this mansion are a number of mosaics and a magnificent room paved in coloured marble *(opus sectile)*, vestiges that were brought to light by the excavations undertaken in the nineteen-seventies by José Álvarez Sáenz de Buruaga and the more recent ones fomented by the Regional Government of Extremadura.

No sooner has the visitor reached the end of the paved remains of the Roman road than he comes face to face with the sturdy rubblework fabric of the original town wall, which, probably at a later date, was reinforced at its most vulnerable points by the addition of solid granite ashlars.

On the left as one descends the path lies the most important monument of the whole *alcazaba*, namely

**89.** *The Alcazaba. Roman houses (4th century A.D.).*

**90.** *Passageway
in the dungeon.*

its *aljibe* or underground water deposit, which is commonly referred to as *Baño de la Reina* or Queen´s Bath. Possibly of Roman origin, the deposit provided the fortress with a continuous supply of water that was filtered from the adjacent river Guadiana. It owes its present-day appearance to the work of the Moslems, who employed an abundance of Roman and Visigothic material in its construction. In order to enter the deposit one passes through a pair of jambs made from Visigothic marble pilasters decorated with plant motifs and out onto a landing, from where a further series of pilasters acting as jambs and lintels open up the way down a double staircase –large enough for horses to pass through– to the lower level of the *aljibe,* which is on the same level as the river and is protected by magnificent barrel vaulting fashioned in granite ashlars taken from former Roman buildings and partly supported by a beautiful Visigothic pilaster crowned by a Lower Empire capital.

If the visitor wishes, he may round off his visit to the *alcazaba* by going up onto the top of the walls, from where he will be able to see the entire length of the Roman bridge and in particular the truly Augustan section of the same, that which ends at the first of the pathways leading down from the bridge.

From up on the walls we can also appreciate the sheer strength of the Roman dyke that lies down at our feet and which was built to protect the town against flooding at times when the river would break its banks. Indeed, the outer wall of the Moslem fortress was laid right along the top of this dyke, whose structure is one of solid rubblework.

The *alcazaba,* which in times gone by was completely hidden by modern constructions (up until the sixties it was merely an orchard), is gradually recovering its original aspect thanks, on the one hand, to the expropriation orders issued on the houses built against it on the outside, and, on the other, to the systematic excavation campaigns being undertaken on the inside, which, if they continue, will surely uncover not only a large section of the original town wall, but also an entire residential district of the Late Roman Empire and possibly one or other civil or ecclesiastical buildings from the Visigothic era.

We can finish off our visit by admiring, in the north-western corner of the *alcazaba*, the monastery that was established by the knights of the Order of St James upon the reconquest of the town by Alfonso IX in the year 1228. At first the knights adapted this section of the fortress for use as the headquarters of their Order, but subsequently converted it into a monastery. To this end, they added the following elements: a beautiful keep; a two-storeyed cloister featuring semicircular arches springing from simple-based columns, smooth shafts and –in some cases– Ionic capitals; a church and some ancillary outbuildings. The whole monastery complex was to be severely damaged in the battles fought between the supporters of Isabella *La Católica* and those of Juana *La Beltraneja*, in the skirmishes between Marshal Soult and the Duke of Wellington, and finally in the fighting that took place here at the outset of the Spanish civil war. Nowadays the monastery, after having been subjected to an arduous restoration programme, is the seat of the *Junta* or Regional Government of Extremadura and can be visited by using the entrance situated on the *Plaza del Rastro*.

# MODERN MÉRIDA

## BASILICA OF *SANTA EULALIA*

According to popular legend, this basilica was erected in the early 4th century on the site where St Eulalie was martyrized during Diocletian´s persecution of Christians (in the year 304). Its original structure, portrayed by the poet Prudencio in a passionate, poetic style in his work entitled *Peristephanon ("clad in shining marble, covered by golden roofs and paved in rich mosaics, reminiscent of a green meadow dotted with brightly coloured flowers"),* and the subsequent alterations carried out by archbishop Fidel (560-571) and recorded by Paulo Diácono in his work on the Fathers of Mérida, were completely eradicated during the period of Moslem domination, not a single vestige having survived to the present point in time.

Generally speaking, the present-day appearance of the basilica is to be traced back to the reconstruction that the edifice underwent in the course of the 13th century after the town had been conquered by Christian forces in 1230. The features that still remain of this primitive, unsophisticated Romanesque structure are its plan (that of a typical basilica, featuring a nave and two aisles, the former being the most spacious, and no crossing), and the three apses to be found at its sanctuary, which are semicircular in shape on the inside and square on the outside. Other elements dating from this early period are one of the doorways lining the southern façade –the one that, leading into

**91.** *Excavations underway at the Church of Santa Eulalia.*

**92.** *Santa Eulalia. Romanesque portal.*

the crossing, comprises a splayed opening with horseshoe arches and archivolts, the latter resting on small marble-shafted columns– and the doorway of the western façade, which today is walled up due to the adjoining convent and which features the same characteristics as the southern facing one, although this one is more stylized, as indeed are the doors giving access to the side apses.

The interior of the basilica is supported by means of four thick central piers. Two of these are cylindrical, whilst the other two are of an irregular cruciform shape, each of them featuring four attached columns with capitals dating from different epochs on which a series of pointed arches rest. As far as the basilica roofing is concerned, a mixture is to be observed of wooden structures (in its 16th-century second and third sections) and the Gothic ribbed and barrel vaulting of the crossing.

The presbytery, which apparently also belongs to the Gothic period, is framed by a large ogival arch springing from two massive columns with Roman capitals and above which there is a large Romanesque window.

Today just three side chapels survive in the basilica interior, one situated next to the epistle and another two on either side of the lower choir.

Of the alterations made to the church in later periods, we should draw special attention to the wooden roof to be found in the central section just before the choir, which still retains its octagonal Mudéjar framework, and the second doorway of the southern façade which, Isabelline in style (16th-century), has two distinguishable bodies. The first of these, the lower one, features a splayed open doorway with a depressed trefoil arch, whereas the second, upper section affords a splayed opening formed by a semicircular arch and framed by sophisticated beading.

We should also highlight, amongst the retables and sculptures that lie in the possession of the church, the 18th-century Churrigueresque retable adorning the main altar and two sculpted images, one of which, portraying the Most Holy Christ of the Remedies, is the work of the 16th-century Castilian school, whereas the other, Our Father Jesus of Nazareth, has been attributed to the Granada school of the 18th century.

### The Excavations

Taking advantage of the resurfacing work being carried out on the church floor, the Department of Education and Culture of the Regional Government of Extremadura has promoted a series of archaeological investigations that have unearthed an impressive collection of remains which will help us to resolve quite a few of the mysteries surrounding the history of the original building.

Research carried out to date has confirmed the earliest remains found at the excavation as originating from Roman times and belonging either to a private dwelling or to a water-containing structure that once occupied the entire site of the present-day church and of which remains of stoups, water deposits and hydraulic floorings still survive. To be attributed to the Palaeochristian era (4th and 5th centuries A.D.) are two mausoleums, one of which still retains on its roof the remains of its original mosaic decoration. Set out around the said mausoleums is a series of smaller structures which could well have been places of worship dedicated to the early Christian martyrs, such as St Eulalie, to whom one such structure was probably devoted. Finally, sturdy granite ashlar foundations have been discovered that are to be assigned to the Visigothic period. Theoretically they would seem to belong to the work on the enlargement of the basilica carried out by archbishop Fidel and related in the writings of Paulo Diácono. Also pertaining to this era are the abundant remains of sarcophagi and marble tomb slabs, along with the vestiges of another mausoleum featuring a mosaic and an agape table.

### CONVENT OF SANTA OLALLA

Lying adjacent to the church with which it shares its name, and even concealing the original Romanesque portal situated at the foot of the latter, is the convent that once belonged to the friars of St Eulalie. The first stages of its construction having been begun in around 1530, work on the convent building was not to be concluded until well into the 18th century. The main body of the building is an L-shaped structure surrounded by a cloister and ancillary buildings. The most noble feature of the convent is a beautiful mirador or balcony with large openings formed by Doric half-columns. Amongst the materials used in the construction of the convent were dimension stone –employed in the portals and arches–, certain re-used elements and earth-filled bricks. Whereas the most important parts of the building (situated in its eastern wing) are covered by barrel vaulting, the rest of the structure features wooden roofing. Apart from the time when it was to become an unexpected royal residence during the visit of the king and queen to Mérida, the convent had had a rather unstable existence when it was deprived of its religious function during the process of ecclesiastical disentailment. Subsequently, the building came into the hands of private individuals who were to use it for a number of different purposes. Until very recently it served as a timber yard.

## CONVENT OF *SAN ANDRÉS*

This convent was erected in 1571 on the orders of local citizen Francisco de Vargas, although in reality work on its construction did not finish until the year 1636. The only elements remaining of its original structure, which over the years has both deteriorated greatly and undergone many alterations, are the church, which today has been converted into a store, and the façade presiding the *Plaza de Santo Domingo.*

Baroque in style, the church has a rectangular plan with no apse, and measures 7.6 metres by 13.65 metres. Its central area is barrel-vaulted, as are the presbytery and the final section of the church body, which also feature lunettes. The best-preserved of its façades, that which gives onto *Plaza Santo Domingo,* consists of brick walls faced with lime mortar that rest on granite ashlar bases. The centre of the façade is graced by an elegant Tuscan granite portal featuring two columns on either side of its opening and an entablature complete with cornice. Situated above the cornice is a niche holding the marble image of St Dominic and the emblem of his Order with the following motto: *"Defendere Fidei ordo veritatis".*

The convent itself, which even prior to *desamortización* or the process of ecclesiastical disentailment had long fallen into decline, was subsequently abandoned and used for a number of different civil purposes, as a result of which it was to undergo a series of far-reaching alterations which have reduced it to its present-day condition. By means of a decree issued on the 10th February 1989, the convent was declared a national cultural asset, and at present it awaits the assignment of a more honourable use, in keeping with its brilliant past.

## CONVENT-HOSPITAL
## OF JESUS OF NAZARETH

This convent was founded in around the year 1724 –even though it was not completed until ten years later– by the Brothers of Jesus of Nazareth, who belonged to the tertiary Franciscan order that was

**93.** *Interior of the Jesus of Nazareth Hospital, today a state-run hotel or parador.*

created in 1673 by the priest from Mérida Father Cristóbal de Santa Catalina with the aim of taking care of convalescent patients who had no financial resources.

The site chosen for the convent was the *Plazuela de Santiago,* and it was built using the remains that were scattered about the surrounding area, some of which belonged to ancient Roman buildings of the Provincial Forum, and even some load-bearing elements taken from an old mosque, judging by the Arabic characters engraved on some of the cloister columns. In the course of the 18th century, the convent-hospital was to become the focal point of intense activity, and it even saw the establishment –at the hands of prior Domingo de Nuestra Señora– of a centre for ancient artefacts, which in time would prove to be the nucleus of the future Archaeological Museum. However, owing to

**94.** *Portal of the convent of the Sisters of the Immaculate Conception.*

**95.** *Portal of the Church of Nuestra Señora del Carmen.*

mounting financial difficulties, the convent was to fall into decline in the early 19th century and indeed was abandoned during the War of Independence. Upon the conclusion of hostilities, a programme of restoration work was carried out on the building that was not to finish until 1837. Not long afterwards, in 1839, the convent was finally abandoned and was brought under civil jurisdiction, as a result of which it was subsequently used first as a mental hospital and then a civilian prison.

The best-preserved parts of its original structure –which has been totally changed due to the work that was done on the building as from 1927 in order to adapt it to the rôle of a *Parador Nacional de Turismo* or state-run hotel– are the cloister and the church. The latter features a rectangular plan with an incipient transept and a total of three semicircular apses, one of which is situated at the sanctuary and the other two on either side of the crossing. The church roofing is barrel-vaulted in the nave and the three apses, and features a dome rising up over pendentives and a lantern over the crossing.

## CHURCH OF *NUESTRA SEÑORA DEL CARMEN*

Founded as it was by the Order of St Francis, this church constitutes a fine example of eighteenth-century religious architecture in Mérida. It has a Latin cross ground plan and features a barrel-vaulted nave and a crossing crowned by a dome. The most outstanding characteristic of the church is its Tuscan façade featuring two hollowed pilasters and a Doric frieze adorned with triglyphs and metopes, from which a broken pediment arises. This pediment houses the second level of the façade which, Ionic in style, is crowned by a pair of busts placed on either side of a coat of arms. The niche containing an image of the Blessed Virgin with Baby Jesus is flanked by the coat of arms of the Order that the church once belonged to and that of the town of Mérida. Ornaments in the shape of scallop shells are seen to lie above both of the said emblems. A commemorative stone right at the top of the façade bears the following inscription: "The first stone of this church and convent was laid on the 26th day of April 1721 and when all work was finished the Holy Sacrament was placed in position on the 19th October 1737. May it be for the glory of God and the Blessed Virgin. Amen."

The interior of the church is of an austere nature and the 19th-century Neoclassical retables, along with the mass-produced sculptures, are of little artistic value.

## CONVENT OF THE SISTERS OF THE IMMACULATE CONCEPTION

The convent belonging to the Order of the Immaculate Conception of Our Lady was founded by Francisco Moreno de Almaraz in 1588. The nuns who were to take charge of the convent came to Mérida from the town of Llerena. The church has a rectangular ground plan and its roofing structure features barrel-vaulting pierced with lunettes and a dome rising up over pendentives crowning a kind of crossing and the presbytery. Turning to the exterior of the church, the upper section of its façade features two flat-arched openings belonging to the convent, whilst opening out from its lower section are the only two portals of the church.

The stone elements of the church façade date from the time of the convent´s foundation. The doorway itself consists of a depressed arch, the spandrels of which feature leaf ornaments, and is framed by embedded columns. Resting on the latter is an entablature with a scallop-shell vaulted niche housing an image of the Blessed Virgin and Baby Jesus.

**96.** *Santa María la Mayor. Christ of the O.*

## CATHEDRAL OF *SANTA MARÍA LA MAYOR*

The Cathedral of *Santa María la Mayor* rises up on the site where in Visigothic times another church of the same name, the metropolitan cathedral of Mérida, once stood. The fabric of the latter edifice having been ruined in the course of time, some details as to part of its structure are nevertheless known thanks to the brief description of it to be found in the precious 6th-century opuscule entitled *"De vita et miraculis Patrum Emeritensium"* (Of the Lives and Miracles of the Father Saints of Mérida). The cathedral of Mérida, which acted as the seat for Councils, was also referred to as the church of *Santa Jerusalén* or Holy Jerusalem. Adjacent to it lay a *basilicula* or small baptistery and an *episcopium* or episcopal palace.

Even though Christian worship was respected when Mérida was subjected to Islamic rule, in time the church itself was to fall into decay and eventually came to lie in ruins. At the beginning of the 13th

**97.** *Cathedral of Santa María la Mayor.*

century, when the town was recaptured from the Moslems by the Christian forces, the church was reconstructed right from its very foundations and re-conferred its original dedication. In this way it took on the aspect that is still to be appreciated today, despite the many subsequent alterations.

The plan of the church features a nave and two aisles –the former being double the width of the latter– separated by piers that are square in section and have an embedded column on each of their faces. A series of pointed arches is seen to spring from the said columns. The ceiling of the nave and aisles, which originally took the form of a Mudéjar wooden framework, is now groin-vaulted.

The presbytery comprises two distinct sections, the first of which features stellar vaulting over a rectangular ground plan, whereas the second is fan-vaulted and has bosses decorated with fleurons and the Lamb of God.

On either side of the presbytery, situated beneath their respective *arcosolia*, one can admire the alabaster tombs of Diego de Vera y Mendoza, *trece* or elected leader of the Order of St James, and his wife, Marina Gómez de Figueroa.

The central apse is decorated with a large retable dating from 1762. The latter consists of two sections and in modern times was deprived of its scallop-shell shaped crowning ornament in order to reveal a 13th-century window that lay behind it.

Resting as it does on a pedestalled base, the central niche corresponding to the second level of the retable holds the image of the divine figure to whom the church is dedicated –the Blessed Virgin Mary– which is accompanied by those of the apostles Peter and Paul and the Mérida´s own saints, Eulalie and Julia.

The most outstanding of the apsidal chapels is that on the Epistle side, known as the chapel of the Counts of La Roca, which is divided into two sections, both of which are groin-vaulted, one of its bosses being graced by the crenellated coat of arms of the patrons of the chapel. Standing in all its resplendence in the chapel situated on the Gospel side is the impressive carved figure of Christ of the O, a magnificent work of religious imagery dating from the mid-14th century.

Worthy of special note amongst the burial chapels are the one belonging to Cecilia de Mendoza, dating from the first third of the 16th century, and the one built at the behest of the *conquistador* from Mérida, Moreno de Almaraz.

The eastern façade, lying as it does at the foot of the church structure, is the work of the master architect Mateo Sánchez de Villaviciosa. It has two sections or levels, the lower one of which features double hollowed Ionic pilasters, whilst the upper one boasts fluted Corinthian pilasters framing the coats of arms of Mérida and the Order of St James.

Both the said sections are seen to support an entablature, the one corresponding to the second level being crowned by a cornice, above which stands a flat-arched balconied opening. Engraved on the entablature is the following Psalm of David: *"Domum tuam Domine Sanctitudo. Ps. LXXXII."*

The church owes its southern façade, the one that gives out onto the square, to the pious endeavour of Moreno de Almaraz. Work on its construction was completed in 1579. Lying in its niche is the alabaster image of *Nuestra Señora de la Guía* (Our Lady of the Way), to whom travellers would commend themselves before setting of on their journeys, especially those who were heading for the Americas.

## THE PALACE OF MENDOZA

The only palace remaining today in the town of Mérida, the one that belonged to the Counts –later to become the Dukes– of La Roca and which had disappeared by the end of the 19th century, is the one that in its day was the property of Luis de Mendoza, who had married a lady of the Vera family, who was herself the true owner of the building.

The palace features two façades, the main one, which has a southern orientation and looks out onto the square, and another that faces west. Their fabric, which reveals two different periods of construction, is composed of re-used Roman ashlars.

The construction of the palace building goes back as far as the 15th century. We are informed of this by the Late Gothic style of a beautiful window featuring three trefoil arches and marble mullions with capitals bearing little shields, as well as that of two smaller windows with ogee arches. In the late 16th century or early 17th century, the façade was remodelled in keeping with the taste prevailing at that time. Thus, a continuous balcony was introduced spanning three flat-arched openings, two of which feature curved pediments and flank the third, which has a triangular pediment that is broken at its apex in order to make room for a coat of arms that is quartered to represent the Vera family and their alliances.

The said coat of arms is mounted on the breast of an eagle that holds in its beak a *phylacteria* or band with the inscription *"Veritas Vincit"*, the heraldic motto of the Counts of La Roca. Each of the pediments is crowned by a series of spheres, pyramids and cups.

**98.** *Palace of Mendoza.*

Lying beneath the Gothic window is a doorway that could well have been the original entrance to the palace and which today has been converted into a large-sized window. Its pediment ends up in scrolls, whilst the coat of arms, supported by an eagle, displays the arms of the Vera, Tovar, Zúñiga and Ovando families. As is the case with the other coat of arms gracing the façade, this one also appears superimposed over a cross of St James.

The interior of the palace, which has undergone far-reaching alterations, has a courtyard surrounded by a cloister with galleries, only one of which belongs to the original design of the building, the other three, featuring Tuscan columns, having been the result of a modification undertaken possibly in the 17th century.

## CHURCH OF *SANTA CLARA*

The Church of *Santa Clara* was founded as part of the convent for the nuns of the Order of St Clare by Dr Lope Sánchez de Triana, their patron, in the year 1602. Estebanillo González, the renowned *pícaro* or rogue, is

90

**99.** *Church of Santa Clara.*

known to have taken part in the work on its construction. The fabric of the church is generally composed of brickwork interspersed with square sections of rubble, with the exception of the façade at the foot of the church, which is entirely made of rubblework.

The socles, doorways and window frames are fashioned in granite, some of the stone blocks bearing the mark of the mason who dressed them.

The Tuscan eastern portal is formed by two columns supporting an entablature whose pediment is broken by a niche holding the image of *Nuestra Señora de la Antigua,* a sculpture that once was kept in the convent that shares its name. Above the said niche is another architectural level which, supported by small pilasters, features a broken pediment encompassing an emblem portraying the three nails from Christ´s crucifixion superimposed by the initial IHS.

The western portal, which gives onto the Plaza de Santa Clara, is similar to the former in structure, but less sophisticated.

On display inside the church is an impressive collection of Visigothic remains of Mérida.

**100.** *Hermitage of Nuestra Señora de la Antigua.*      **101.** *Convent Church of St James.*

## HERMITAGE OF *NUESTRA SEÑORA DE LA ANTIGUA*

This hermitage originally formed part of the old convent of the same name which, belonging to the Franciscan discalced monks, was established in around the year 1676. The convent having been abandoned by the first half of the 18th century, its remains were to firstly house the premises of a washing house for wool, and subsequently hold a tannery for animal skins. Practically all that is still to be seen today of the original hermitage fabric is its Gothic-style church which, built in the late 16th and early 17th centuries, features walls of poorly hewn ashlars and a rectangular ground plan with a non-projecting sanctuary.

The roof of the church, possibly the most significant aspect of the whole building, comprises two stellar vaults held up by six compound pillars on the inside and six sturdy buttresses on the outside. The church opens out to the exterior by means of two portals, one of which is situated at its foot and features a depressed trefoil arch and rusticated masonry, whilst the other lies on the Epistle side and displays a segmental arch with a fluted archivolt, the pattern of which is carried on down its jambs. The opening has a square frame which is formed by the continuation of the last flute of the jamb and a cornice, on top of which are a pair of pinnacles, one on either side. Placed in between the said pinnacles and enclosed by another cornice is a flat-arched opening. The whole façade is crowned by brick openwork tracery.

Having been recently acquired by the Mérida town council, this building nowadays houses a cultural centre.

**102.** *The modern bridge "Lusitania".*

93

# INDEX

HISTORICAL INTRODUCTION ........................................................................................... 3

PRE-ROMAN MÉRIDA ................................................................................................... 15
    The Megalithic Sepulchre at Lácara ........................................................................ 16
    The Cave at La Calderita .......................................................................................... 16
    The Cave Art Ensemble at San Serván ..................................................................... 17

ROMAN MÉRIDA .......................................................................................................... 17
    Topography and Urban Development of Roman Mérida ......................................... 17
    Buildings Devoted to Public Spectacles .................................................................. 23
        *The Theatre* .......................................................................................................... 23
        *The Amphitheatre* ............................................................................................... 27
        *The Circus* ............................................................................................................ 30
    The National Museum of Roman Art ...................................................................... 33
        *Ground Floor* ....................................................................................................... 38
        *Middle Floor* ........................................................................................................ 42
        *Upper Floor* .......................................................................................................... 42
    The Santa Eulalia Monument .................................................................................. 46
    Temple of Mars ....................................................................................................... 47
    Thermae Building in *Calle Reyes Huertas* ............................................................. 49
    Forum Portico .......................................................................................................... 49
    Trajan´s Arch ........................................................................................................... 51
    The Temple of Diana ............................................................................................... 53
    The Roman Houses .................................................................................................. 55
        *The House of the Amphitheatre* ......................................................................... 55
        *Casa del Mitreo or House of the Mithraeum* ...................................................... 58
    The Bridge over the River Guadiana ........................................................................ 61
    The Bridge over the River Albarregas ....................................................................... 63
    The Little Roman Bridge .......................................................................................... 63
    Aqueducts and Reservoirs ....................................................................................... 64
        *The Cornalvo Aqueduct* ...................................................................................... 65
        *The San Lázaro Aqueduct* ................................................................................... 67
        *The Proserpina Aqueduct known as"Los Milagros"* ........................................... 69
    The Roman Baths at Alange .................................................................................... 72

CHRISTIAN MÉRIDA ..................................................................................................... 75
    The Visigothic Collection ........................................................................................ 75
    The Palaeochristian Basilica at *Casa Herrera* ....................................................... 78

MOSLEM MÉRIDA ........................................................................................................ 79
    The *Alcazaba* or fortress ....................................................................................... 79

MODERN MÉRIDA ........................................................................................................ 82
    Basilica of *Santa Eulalia* ....................................................................................... 82
    *The Excavations* .................................................................................................... 84
    Convent of *Santa Olalla* ....................................................................................... 84
    Monastery of *San Andrés* ..................................................................................... 85

Jesus of Nazareth Monastery-Hospital ............................................................................................... 85
Church of *Nuestra Señora del Carmen* .............................................................................................. 87
Convent of the Sisters of the Third Franciscan Order, the Immaculate Conception ......................... 87
Cathedral of *Santa María la Mayor* ................................................................................................... 88
The Palace of Mendoza ...................................................................................................................... 89
Church of *Santa Clara* ...................................................................................................................... 90
Hermitage of *Nuestra Señora la Antigua* .......................................................................................... 93

PRACTICAL INFORMATION ABOUT MÉRIDA ..................................................................................... 95